SECRET ORIGINS

MAYA DANIELS

Vinci Books

vinci-books.com

Published by Vinci Books Ltd in 2026

1

Copyright © Maya Daniels 2020

The author has asserted their moral right to be identified as the author of this work in accordance with the Copyright, Designs and Patents Act 1988. This work is a work of fiction. Names, characters, places and incidents are the product of the author's imagination or are used fictitiously. Any resemblance to actual persons, living or dead, places and incidents is entirely coincidental.

All rights reserved. No part of this publication may be copied, reproduced, distributed, stored in any retrieval system, or transmitted in any form or by any means, including photocopying, recording, or other electronic or mechanical methods, nor used as a source for any form of machine learning including AI datasets, without the prior written permission of the publisher.

The publisher and the author have made every effort to obtain permissions for any third party material used in this book and to comply with copyright law. Any queries in this respect should be brought to the attention of the publisher and any omissions will be corrected in future editions.

A CIP catalogue record for this book is available from the British Library.

Paperback ISBN: 9781036705886

The EU GPSR authorised representative is Logos Europe, 9 rue Nicolas Poussion, 17000 La Rochelle, France contact@logoseurope.eu

By Maya Daniels

The Courtless Fae Series
Secret Origins

The Necronomicon Guardian
The Magician
The High Priestess

Chronicles of Forbidden Witchery
Resting Witch Face
Pitch a Witch
Witch Please
Payback is a Witch

The Broken Halos Series
The Devil is in the Details
Speak of the Devil
Encounter with the Devil
The Devil in Disguise
To Look the Devil in the Eye
Better The Devil You Know
Give a Devil His Due

The Last Note Series
Sound
Sonata

Hidden Portals Trilogy
Venus Trap
The First Secret

Daywalker Series
Investigated
Infiltrated
Instigated
Initiated
Infuriated
Ignited

Infernal Regions for the Unprepared
Black Hand
Lower World
Everlasting Fire
Place of Torment
Hellfire To Come

New Blood Rising
Rebirth - Risorgimento
Overthrown - Rovesciamento
Recognition - Riconoscimento

The Gatekeepers Legacy
Legacy of Water
Legacy of Fire
Legacy of Spirit

Honor Among Thieves

Stolen Magic

Stolen Oath

By Maya Daniels

The Cursed Kingdom

Prologue

Trust: a fickle thing that could mess you up for life if given to the wrong people. It also happened to be the story of my life, or as much of it as I could remember anyway.

The beautiful sound of the rain splattering the glass windows was suffocated by the low hum of conversations and the droning of the annoying country tune playing through the speakers in the crowded pub. Some song about the guy whispering to his horse about the girl getting away or something. I would've preferred the horse over the person, but what did I know? Leaning with both elbows on the polished bar, I watched the glass of rum and coke cradled between my palms with such fascination one might think it was hiding the greatest wisdom of all times. Everything around me was muted to white noise as all thoughts were pushed to some deep recess of my brain where they'd leave me alone, even if it was just for a moment. I'd struggled to quiet the urgency of my mind, which pulled me in every direction most of my life, but then I discovered that sitting in this particular shithole brought the elusive silence I'd been searching for.

Who would've thought being around humans was a good thing?

Not me, that was for sure.

So much had happened so far that I could've sworn my mind had started short-circuiting because it was unable to process the sheer volume of disasters piling up one after the other. I knew Alexius—my boss and the Daywalker vampire that took a chance on me when I was about to run and hide from the supernatural world—was up to something. I recognized the signs immediately, from the elusive half answers to his carefully picked assignments for me that were not the norm. I was his right hand, his hit man—or hitwoman if you will—doing all his dirty work until I wasn't anymore. When the secrecy started, I should've listened to my gut and followed the jerk, but I was trying to work on my insecurities, so I gave him the benefit of the doubt. Many people died. More will die, too, and all because I let my guard down and trusted someone.

And there was that damn word trust, again.

What a fucking joke.

"Is this seat taken?" The voice coming from my right wasn't one I'd heard before, so I reluctantly dragged my eyes away from the object sitting between my cupped palms to look at the shmuck. I even managed not to grind my teeth or snarl like a feral beast at the poor thing. Look at me adulting.

"It is."

The rejection entered one ear and exited the other before I had time to blink. Interest sparked in the darkness of his eyes, which looked me up and down slow enough I had no doubt he could become my new tailor, no measurements needed. You'd think my dismissal of him was an invitation for a quickie in one of the bathrooms that had seen better days. His square jaw with a couple days' worth of stubble on it and that slightly crooked nose rested on an attractive enough face, for a human at least. His features added up to someone I'd definitely take for a ride on any given day ... just not today. Unfortunately, humans had deviated from their primal natures so much that the poor creature beside me couldn't rely on his intuition, which should be warning him about the predator before him. Instead of being scared of me, he actually smirked as if I was amusing.

I smirked back.

"Whatever it is that you are thinking at this very moment, it will not end well for you boy." My comment made the amusement slip off his face, but it didn't deter him any further than that. "Go find a nice girl who will give you an even nicer blow job so you can fall asleep with a smile on your face." His lips parted, but I was not in the mood to hear what would come out from between them. "If I put a smile on your face, it'll be of the permanent kind. The one I'll carve into your skin, one that will give the coroner nightmares for years. We don't want that now, do we? It also makes a poor canvas for postmortem makeup. Foundation for dead people is expensive, trust me."

"You are a crazy bitch!" he spat the words at me with disgust. Unfortunately, not even a little fear showed as he rushed away to whichever hole he'd crawled out of.

"Why, thank you kindly," I called after him, smiling from ear to ear. It made his legs move faster, but he kept glancing over his shoulder as if he expected me to start stalking him. As tempting as that idea was, I really was not in the mood. All I wanted was to mope in peace.

A girl had a right to brood, too.

Especially if she'd been screwed over too many times to count through no fault of her own by people or the Fates themselves.

She had a right to kill the motherfuckers, too. Too bad some of them were already dead.

"You promised not to scare people in the pub, Myst." The bartender scowled at me, the light sheen of sweat gathered around his hairline and upper lip stood out against his pale skin while he nervously wiped his trembling hands on his apron. "You done with that one?" It's not always a good thing when the bartender knows your name.

The middle-aged human tending the bar jerked his chin at my rum and coke from the other side of the long, wooden slab, not daring to come closer. No, this one was not from the smart stock, he just had the misfortune of seeing me kill a demon in the back alley one night while he was dumping the trash. He'd emptied his bladder, and I'd honestly been surprised he didn't have a heart attack right then and there. He stood frozen for a few seconds before he bolted inside and locked the back door. I followed him and discovered that this pub silenced the thoughts tormenting my mind, so we had a long chat that night. He kept my secret, and I let him live. We were buddies now. I didn't know his name, though. I never asked, and he never offered. It worked well for me if I ever changed my mind and decided to kill him. I hated knowing the name of the people I killed.

"If I didn't know better, I might think you were trying to get me drunk and take advantage of me." I grinned to show him I was joking, but the blood drained from his face making him even paler. "It's a joke." I deadpanned frowning, and he relaxed.

Humans were very strange creatures.

He scuttled away the second I shook my head to decline his offer for another drink. I hadn't touched the one I had since, thanks to the brave guy who tried his luck with me tonight, the silence in my head had disappeared. Being barely above five foot two made men think I was approachable. They'd think twice if they knew I was a creature of the night who washed her hands with blood on a daily basis. Even the supernaturals were scared of me. Everyone feared what they didn't understand, and no one had a clue what I was.

Not even me.

Apart from the fact that I was Fae, and after spending time at the Daywalker Academy in Sienna appointed as one of the Courtless, I had no memory of my origin. The only thing I could remember was opening my eyes when I found myself on the steps of the Academy stretched out in front of the double doors like day-old roadkill someone dumped there. I had no memories of my past, where I came from, or how I got there. Soren, the ancient Dragon Blood, made sure they took me in, but the moment the Order started to poke around in my forgotten past, some unknown instinct inside me reared its head and made me run. For all the good it did me. I had other reasons I ran from Sienna, too, but I didn't want to think about that. About him.

Coming across Francesca Drake, a half blood with a very strong Fae bloodline, woke something else in my psyche. The darkness I felt in her called to my own like a beacon of hope. I wanted to hate the female since she was the reason for half of my troubles, but it was difficult to hate Francesca. More powerful than anyone else I'd known, the girl was as naïve as she was dangerous. But she grew on me like a virus I couldn't detect, and before I knew it, all I wanted to do was protect her, or die trying, as she ran head-first into danger. It stirred something powerful and ravenous in me, a hunger to learn why I couldn't remember anything before finding myself in Sienna. Did I go there on my own because I was running from something? Or did someone knock me out and wipe my brain before discarding me like yesterday's news?

After the betrayal Alexius served me like cold porridge to a starving peasant, anger simmered and churned in my gut, spurring on my need to find answers. I might not know what type of a creature I was, but I knew one thing: if Death himself came across me, he'd think twice before raising a hand. So, with that being said, if I had been running at the time ... who had I been running from, and how could I find them? And if I was discarded by someone in Sienna for whatever reason ... who was it that thought fucking with my head would be a good idea, and where could I find them?

Because one thing was certain, one way or another: I would find them.

Lifting the now-warm glass full of rum and coke, I took a slow sip, eyeing the human bartender who was pretending not to watch me from the corner of his eye. Tonight was *"The"* night, the moment when the hunted becomes a hunter and heads would start to roll. I was done allowing people to mess with me. The time for playing nice—even if nice was relative in my case—or pretending to be human was long past. There was no cure for my insanity. The blood boiling in my veins craved violence, and the longer it waited to get what it wanted, the worse things would become. A sleeping monster had awakened inside me and it was getting stronger by the minute. I must discover who and what I was. For my sake, but also for everyone else's. I had a feeling the path to that discovery would have a pretty solid body count. Never, not even for a second, did I wonder why that thought made me smile.

Little did I know at that time that what I was searching for had started looking for me, too.

Chapter One

Drumming my fingers on the steering wheel of the SUV, I watched the raindrops dance over the windshield in the dark parking lot of the abandoned warehouse. The brightness of the fog lights was devoured by the pitch black of the night illuminating only a small portion of the moistened packed dirt and potholes, which were filling up with more water by the second. We hadn't had that much rain in this city in years. It was a nice change from the suffocating heat. It was good to enjoy it while we could. I might've arrived at the meeting place early, but I'd rather wait than walk into a set up. No one had ever said Myst was not prepared.

The sound of rain always calmed me, but when my breathing was bouncing off the interior of the car and so loud it was the only thing I could hear, I felt a little on edge. It might've been the anticipation of what I was doing, too. I had to start somewhere, so I made the call without a second thought. Approaching things after I'd looked at all the pros and cons of the situation was my go-to, at least until tonight. I'd blame it on the rum I sucked up in the dingy bar, kind of like how the Sahara would soak up this rain if it had the chance.

A shadow from the side disturbed the stream of yellow light stretching a yard or so in front of the car, and I tightened my hands on the steering wheel. Keeping my shoulders relaxed, I held my breath and let all my senses tune in to my surroundings. It was too early for the person I called to be here, so it was either someone else, or this was about to become a trap gone wrong for them. Shifting in my seat, I adjusted my foot on the gas pedal, preparing to slam it down the second someone not meant to be here stepped into the light. It wouldn't kill them if it was a supernatural, but it'd slow them down enough so I could do the job with my own hands. I did love my job.

The passenger door was ripped open none to gently, which amplified the sound of the pouring rain. Releasing the steering wheel, I flipped to the side and kicked out at the same time, pressing my back hard on the door, not stopping even when the door handle dug into my spine. The thin heel of my knee-high boot passed an inch from the familiar but startled face as Leo, a wolf shifter and a damn Daywalker, jerked to the side just in time to avoid being stabbed with it in the middle of his forehead. Being five foot two helped a lot in situations like that. I could twist around in the large vehicle however I wanted.

"Nice to see you too, Myst." Snickering, he batted my foot aside, climbing into the car.

"Why are you here?" Annoyed, I didn't move my leg away; I just adjusted my aim by bending my knee so the tip of the heel was now pressed on his temple. I had every intention to stab him with it if he pissed me off.

"I don't mind playing rough, but I need this head"—He

gingerly took hold of the heel and swiped my foot away from his head—"so the other head can work."

"I'm not interested in your cock, wolf." Huffing, I pulled my leg away and settled back into the car seat.

"That's what they all say at first." Smirking, he wiggled his eyebrows at me, and I snorted despite being frustrated with him.

"What do you want?" My eyes darted to the sickly green light of the clock on the dashboard telling me I had ten or fifteen minutes before my meeting was supposed to take place. "And how did you find me?" Turning my narrowed gaze his way, I made sure he understood I didn't appreciate him tracking me down.

Leo tapped his nose, his smirk growing bigger as my eyes turned into slits. "Okay, fine." He chuckled. "I had a bit of help. Fenrir found—"

"Is he here?" I cut him off as I stiffened in my seat.

"No." The Alpha eyed me as if he expected me to explode at any moment. "Listen, I know there is bad blood between you two, but if you just talk—"

"If that male gets anywhere near me, you'll get him back, sure, but he'll be slit from his throat to his navel. Am I clear?"

"Myst …"

"Am. I. Clear?" I glared at him as I pushed the words through my bared teeth.

"Crystal." Blowing out a tired sigh, Leo slumped next to me. "He knows, that's why I'm here. Fenrir only found the trail so I could track you."

"Why are you here?" The clock told me I had nine, ten minutes max to get the shifter out of here.

"Things happened back in Sienna, and we need your help," Leo whispered after a long stretch of silence, shifting uncomfortably and staring out the windshield without looking my way. "Francesca needs your help ... please."

I really, really didn't want to have anything to do with them. It was a general rule I'd made for myself. A rule that, like an idiot, I kept breaking. The meeting tonight was supposed to help me get going with my own quest, the one to find out what in the world I actually was, and that made the Daywalkers the least of my problems. Fenrir, the asshole that he was, and most probably Zoltan too since he was certainly encouraging him, sent Leo here on purpose. The Alpha was known to be too proud to ask for help. He would demand it, but he never asked for it the way he was now. With a heavy sigh, I let my head hang low on my shoulders.

"I have things to do tonight." I knew I'd regret it, but I couldn't find it in me to turn him down. Having the Alpha owe me a favor could come in handy soon enough. "I'll find you tomorrow and we can see what kind of help you need ..." The clock told me the shifter needed to be out of here in five minutes. "And if I can give it."

"That's all I ask. For you to hear me out." Leo was not a stupid male. He knew something was up since he was already opening the door, the rain getting loud again and soaking up his hair and clothing that had halfway dried while we'd been talking. Raindrops were trickling like rivulets over his face in seconds. My mouth twisted in frustration at the wet car seat he left behind, but he only snickered at my grimace. "I'll pay for the cleaning." With a wink, he slammed the door.

"You better believe you will," I murmured, though I had no doubt he'd heard me.

Tiredly sighing, I tilted my head back and closed my eyes. *Why are you doing this to yourself, you idiot?* I had no answer to my question, but I suspected it could only be one thing:

loneliness, the most powerful motivator. It was what made me become Alexius's lap dog, what pushed me to do his dirty work. It was the same thing that made me sit in the deserted parking lot tonight, as well as what made me agree to help the Alpha. I sat like that for a long time, forgetting everything but the gaping hole inside me.

I was tired of being alone.

I was tired of not knowing.

The shift in the charged air alerted me of a presence I'd only felt twice in my life. My lids opened slowly as I straightened in the car seat, my eyes locking on the shadow of a large man standing in front of the SUV bathed in the yellow light. The fog lights bounced off his dark clothing, casting shadows over his barely visible features. He was alone, something I could tell by the way every muscle on his body was coiled tight as if ready to spring into action at any given moment. I could feel his gaze locked on me even when I knew there was no way he could see that well in the darkness with those bright lights aimed at his face. I fingered the leather braided bracelet on my wrist that I'd hidden from everyone, feeling it vibrate under my fingertips.

"Not yet, buddy. Not just yet." Mumbling under my breath through unmoving lips, I reached for the door and swung it open.

As a bad omen, or maybe a warning from the Fates, lightning split the sky above our heads, flickering ominous ghostly blue light over my companion and me. The thunder boomed a few seconds later, cheering me on for this beginning, or maybe it was screaming at me to turn away and never look back. I ignored it all, my full attention on the man standing stock still in the lights of my car. The thin heels of my boots sunk an inch into the wet ground with each step I took, and by the time I reached him I was soaked to the skin, my leather pants and thin shirt sticking to my skin. My hair was plastered on my head just like his as we regarded each other through wet eyelashes. Amusement danced in his black eyes, which only set off alarms in my head.

"General." My greeting lifted the corners of his thin lips a fraction, which wouldn't have been noticeable if you didn't know the guy.

"Myst," he answered with a barely-there nod of his head. "I should say it's nice to see you, but I'm sure this meeting has nothing to do with exchanging pleasantries."

"I need information." Cutting through the bullshit, I squared my shoulders. That earned me a chuckle.

"And what could I possibly know that you don't?" It unnerved me that he wasn't like any other human. He didn't fidget, shuffle his feet, or even breathe faster in my presence. "It's usually the other way around, our arrangement."

"The information I need is inside my head." Forcing my voice to stay even, I did my best to ignore the slight widening of his eyes. "I need to get it out and it has to be on my terms."

"You need my mage." Not a question but a statement. I said nothing. The mage was not his, but he was the one hiding him from everyone.

Instead of killing the mage I was sent to get out of Alexius's way, I handed him over to the general. The human and I met in a very awkward situation, his life hanging on the line while he faced off with a feral vampire who was running from the hunters. Someone tried to set the general up, but unfortunately for them, my path crossed his just at the right time. The feeling that my boss was up to something was the reason I saved the human's life and gave the mage to him for safekeeping. I needed allies that no one knew about, and there couldn't be a better friend for someone like me than a five-star general in the human military. He had access to most things, all the things I might need one day. Like now.

"Just me and the mage." This made the human shift slightly on his feet. "You can have him back the minute I'm done."

"Alive?" And this was why I liked the general. He knew the right questions to ask, and he knew better than to screw around with me.

"Why would I kill him now after going through the hassle of giving him to you?"

"It depends what he knows after you are done getting your information."

I kept eye contact with him, and he didn't look away. The raindrops were gliding over the deeper wrinkles on his face and dripping from his square chin. With the rain darkening his gray hair and the night somewhat blurring his aged skin, I could see that he'd been a handsome and formidable man in his youth.

"I have ways to make him forget whatever he heard, General. I won't take away your toy." A smile tilted my lips at his frankness.

"He is a living being, not a toy," he reprimanded me in a clipped tone.

"I'll agree when you tell me you don't use him to benefit you." Cocking my head to the side, I blinked away the rain. "You should be retired by now, yet you are at the top of things. I wonder why the humans still keep you around." A muscle was jumping on one side of his jaw as I spoke, which made me snort. "I will use the mage."

"He lives." There was no mistaking the stubborn set of his jaw and shoulders.

"He lives," I answered after a long moment. "I'll let you know the time and the place soon."

With a tight nod, he swiveled on his heel and walked away. My mind was running through possibilities as I stood in the rain as long as it took for me to no longer feel his energy. I saved his life for more than one reason that night. I needed allies, yes, but there was something about the general I hadn't deciphered yet. He was human, but he also wasn't. Not if I could feel his presence the way I always did. That enigma would have to wait for now. I had a ton more pressing matters to deal with.

My leather pants squelched as I jumped back in the car and took off out of the deserted parking lot like the hounds of hell were on my tail. The bracelet vibrated under my skin as if mimicking a chuckle.

Chapter Two

The next day, perched on top of the high wall surrounding an inconspicuous building in the industrial part of the city, I squinted at the thick gray clouds gathering above me. It looked like another day of rain and I couldn't say I was thrilled about it. To add to everything I had on my plate, I was also following the bread crumbs Alexius left behind, so I can find out exactly what he'd done before Francesca killed him. Not because I cared much one way or another, it was more for self-preservation. If he got me mixed up in it, I'd rather know what I was up against.

Shifting on my haunches, I inched further down the wall, silently berating myself for not waiting until the daylight was almost gone. The weather was gloomy and dark, but not enough to hide me if anyone was smart enough to look up. Luckily, for now, the open space around the building was empty, only a handful of cars sat sprinkled around it. Even they were far enough away from one another that I wasn't worried at all. I could handle a handful of people.

The bracelet vibrated on my wrist, as if I needed a reminder that it was there.

I couldn't take the damn thing off. I tried. Cutting it was a whole new nightmare that I didn't want repeated. The phantom pain in my chest almost took my breath away as I swayed on the wall wobbling to the side from that memory. Taking a deep breath, I released it slowly, prying my stiff fingers from the edge of the wall where I was gripping it for dear life. *Snap out of it, fool.* A side door squeaked open in the building, stopping the internal lashing I was about to give myself. Kicking my legs back, I plastered myself on the wall, dragging my body to peek over it. I held my breath as two hunters exited, locking the door behind them before b-lining for one of the larger cars in the lot. They didn't talk, nor did they look at each other as the two unnatural beings disappeared through the metal gates in no time. Clouds of dust billowed from the gravel for a few minutes even after they left. At least I was sure I'd come to the right place.

When no one else came out or made noise, I flipped my legs over the edge and dropped silently on the other side. Keeping my breath even, I sprinted across the open space using the balls of my feet and praying that I wouldn't twist an ankle because of my high-heeled boots. They weren't a fashion statement. No, they were another weapon. My back hit the wall of the building as I reached it, and I waited to see if anyone noticed my presence. From my perch on the wall, I didn't see any surveillance cameras, but I could've missed them if whoever was guarding the place was smart with their placement. When only silence met me for too long, it just proved that arrogance would be the downfall of the supernatural race.

I should know since I had it in spades, too.

This wasn't some mission I was taking. I was only

educating myself on which threats were coming for me so I didn't have to constantly look over my shoulder. At least, that was what I told myself. With that in mind, I glided closer to the closed door on the side of the building and gripped the metal handle. It started moving down on its own and my heart stopped. Not even the "Oh, shit!" I screamed in my head could help me now. There was nowhere to hide and it was too late to run back where I'd come from.

The door swung open.

"Hello boys." Cocking my hip to the side, I gave the two hunters a once over from head to toes, smirking at their startled looks even while my heart was trying to punch a hole through my chest. *You are so stupid. Boys? Really Myst?* I had to agree with the internal asshole that was also me. I totally could've come up with something better than "boys." I was just startled. Yeah, that had to be it.

"I'm expected." Lifting my chin, I looked down—well, since my head only reached their shoulders, it was more up than down—my nose at their silent staring. *Act like you know what you are doing,* I told myself, waiting.

The hunters finally looked at each other, some unspoken conversation happening according to their emotionless faces, not that you could see much of it with the covering hiding everything but their eyes. I waited, not allowing myself to even twitch a muscle. The hunters might be brainless, but even they could pick up on a predator who was about to pounce. No, I needed them unaware if I wanted to get my ass out of this mess. The one on the left nodded mutely and they both stepped aside, allowing me to enter, even holding the door for me.

Aww, they were being gentleman. How sweet.

I decided then and there I'd kill those two last.

My heels echoed, the clicking of the metal on the sterile white tiles bouncing off the equally sterile white walls as I was striding down the long hallway. I never understood the abominations' obsession with white. As if having themselves surrounded by it would wash off the evil that was festering in their veins, which was the complete opposite of me and my love for black. It was better to mask my presence, better to hide so they didn't see me until I slit their throat. I'd never thought too hard on what that said about me, and I had no intention of starting anytime soon either. When I heard the door close, I slowed my stride and glanced over my shoulder to see the two hunters stupidly left me on my own. My eyes darted up and followed the corners of the ceiling to search for cameras.

There were none.

I frowned, turning in a circle. If I didn't decide at the last minute to check this place out I would've thought it was some sort of a ploy. They couldn't have expected me here when I didn't know myself that I'd be standing inside this building tonight. Taking it as a stroke of unexpected luck, I went lurking through every open door I could find. All of them were empty, and the silence through the building was unnerving.

Until the muffled cries reached my ears.

The noise was coming from beneath me, something I would've missed if I didn't stop to examine the hunter's uniform folded neatly on top of a metal hospital grade bed. I knew it was a very bad idea, but I still hurriedly swapped my clothing for the white uniform, rushing out of the room while tugging the face covering over my mouth and nose. At least I left my own garments neatly folded just behind the door. I loved those leather pants and would skin whoever laid a finger on them.

Secret Origins

The search through the never-ending hallways led me to a door with an "employees only" sign that was different than all the rest. If the sign didn't say "hello, come here because this is where we hide important shit,' the metal it was made of would've. I leaned on it and pressed my ear to the cool surface, but it was impossible to hear anything. With an internal curse that should've melted my ears, I grabbed the handle and held it until it melted between my fingers—a neat trick I discovered I could do a while back when I escaped from the Academy.

"Every time there are ominous looking stairs leading down," I told the empty space as I darted down the bottomless stairway.

The cries were getting louder the further I went, until I stopped in my tracks a few steps away from the bottom. Half a dozen hunters turned to face me as one, their soulless gazes locking on my left hand. I glanced down too, then groaned internally. Subconsciously I'd called out my sword. As long as my arm, the light metal blade was glinting happily at me, reflecting the harsh lights. Well shit!

The hunters all moved into their fighting stances, their attention on me.

My foot pivoted to spin me around and take me up the stairs. I knew I was faster than the abominations, and I could be out of there before any of them reached the door to the higher level. That was when something bright yellow caught my attention, dashing out from one of the open doors. My whole body froze when I saw a little girl, around five or six years of age, run straight at the hunters, her little fists pounding on the closest one's thighs. Her blue eyes were too wide on her tear-smudged face, her wavy blonde hair sticking up in all directions, but the little human bared her teeth like she would tear them apart as she kept pounding on the object of her anger. Her bright yellow dress was covered in blood at the front, and it stuck to her little body.

Not your problem, I told myself as I stood frozen like a statue. *You are here for information only.*

The little human kept punching and kicking, but no one paid her attention. Until she opened her little mouth and bit the hunter for all she was worth with her blunt little teeth. I was in awe and quite impressed with her, at least until the abomination swung his arm, catching the little girl on the side of her face and sending her crashing into the wall. Her tiny body crumpled on the floor like a broken doll, but she managed to lift her head and those blue eyes, which were too old to be on that tiny face, locked on me.

"Help my mommy, please."

Goosebumps burst all over my body. I was dressed just like the rest of the hunters and there was no way she could tell the difference. Even the sword couldn't tell a child I wasn't one of the creatures hurting her and her mother. But she kept those eyes on me unblinking, her stare extracting all the air from my lungs.

I couldn't breathe.

The cries started again, so much louder they shredded my insides, yet I stood a few steps away from the bottom locked in the child's stare. *Not my problem,* I tried to convince myself, my body vibrating from my effort to stay put.

"Help her ... please." She hiccupped and her eyes rolled to the back of her head as her little body slumped on the tiles.

"Ah, fuck if it's not my problem now." I snarled, tugging on the leather bracelet around my wrist to release the second biggest pain in my butt.

It felt like there was a tether connecting the bracelet to

the center of my chest and I was tugging my soul loose from my body. It wasn't painful per se, but uncomfortable enough to freak me out each and every time. Black smoke swirled next to me, pulsing and expanding while a thick metal chain formed around my wrist, curling at my feet with a tinkling sound. A black hound the size of a pony materialized to my left, his body vibrating with excitement when the red glowing eyes found the hunters. He hunched down, lowering his head and pinning his ears to the back of his skull, his sharp canines bared at the abominations.

"Have at it Fen." The hound glared at the name I gave him just because he hated it, but he forgot all about it when the hunters moved. I grinned under the face covering, my hunger for violence coming to the surface.

"You fuckers will beg for a death that will never come." With a laugh, I jumped down the few stairs separating me from the hunters and joined my hound.

Chapter Three

Searing pain made my eyes water when the silver star sliced through my upper arm. When me and Fen jumped to join the hunters in the not-so-wide hallway, they spread out to give each other enough room to hurl those damn shuriken they loved so much at us. Short of decapitating me, they couldn't actually kill me, but it was always enough to piss me off. Each hit they scored was like a papercut I didn't know I had until I used hand sanitizer, then it was instant regret as it burned like a bitch for longer than it should.

"Protect the girl." Huffing under my breath at the hound, I ducked under the swinging arm of the hunter to my right.

Blocking the dagger coming from my left with my sword, I spun around slicing a wide circle around me to keep all of them away. Fen's snarl raised the hairs on the back of my neck, then he was sailing through the air over the hunters to land in front of the unconscious girl. The thick chain connecting him to my wrist smacked the closest hunter on the side of his head, making him stagger to the side. No one had ever accused me of not being an opportunist. Using the hunter's dazed state, I skewered him with my sword like a shish kebab, twisting the blade just for the sake of it. The louder he screamed, the more energized I felt.

Another star flew so close to my head I flinched.

The woman cried out with such terror it broke something inside me.

My body and instincts took over. Like a Tasmanian devil, I swirled around the hunters, kicking, punching, and slicing through every piece of them I could reach. Fen was doing his part, his snapping jaws biting chunks of flesh and bone the moment they got within reach, an unusual obedience emanating from him since he wouldn't leave the girl's side. My harsh breath made the air under my face covering hot, as the sterile looking hallways slowly turned into a macabre scene covered in red. Splatters of blood were flung on the pristine walls creating abstract art that satisfied the monster lurking inside me. A humorless smile donned my face, my cheeks hurting from the effort it took to keep it there.

I hated it.

It was over before I knew it, the shouts and screams cutting off so abruptly my ears remained buzzing for a long moment in the sudden silence. Panting, I stood in the middle of a pile of body parts, looking at whatever was left from their white uniforms slowly soaking up the blood from the floor. A thick coppery scent insulted my senses, the covering not enough to protect me from the stench.

The woman whimpered.

It was louder than her screams to my ears.

I was moving before I knew what I was doing. Darting through the open door, I was yanked a few feet inside by the hound's chain. Taking stock, my eyes flicked around the room, the sights curdling the blood in my veins. A woman with a bloody mess of hair covering her face was hunched over a boy around the same age as the little girl lying unconscious in the hallway. A shifter, judging by the stench of him and the fact that he was twice her size, loomed over her as he tried to drag her away from the child. That was when I noticed the scalpel she had clutched in a white-knuckled fist, which she slashed at the shifter with jerky movements before bringing it back to the boy's throat.

"I will kill him before you can take him." Her voice came out low and filled with so much anguish I could barely hear her.

Blue eyes just like the little girl's jerked up over the shifter's shoulder, zooming in on me. Her startled gaze widened as she flicked it over my body. Subconsciously, I tried to take a step toward her only to be yanked back by the chain. When all the color drained from her face, whatever was visible of it through the chunks of hair plastered on it, I remembered what I was wearing and that I was probably more terrifying than the asshole trying to take her child. I was soaked in blood and holding a large sword. The shifter very slowly turned to look over his shoulder.

"Fuck it." I breathed under my nose, and without any sudden movements, I reached up and pulled my hood down.

My hair unraveled and fell around my face, hopefully putting the woman at ease—if anything could put a mother at ease when her child was threatened. It had the desired effect on her, and her body sagged as she listed to the side before catching herself. Though it had a not-so-desired effect on the shifter, who turned to face me with his shoulders bunching up as he prepared to shift. At least there was only one of him, right? The chain tugged on my wrist then, reminding me my movements were limited as long as Fen was connected to me. The one time I actually removed it to set him loose almost killed me. As soon as the connection I had with the hound was gone, I was as good as a mortal. I learned that the hard way.

"Help me, please." She sobbed, her empty hand reaching for me in desperation, her blood-covered fingers trembling with the effort. "You can have my life, just please save my child."

I glanced from her hope-filled eyes to the chain on my wrist.

"You are stupid, Myst," I told myself on a sigh, grabbing ahold of the chain. "You deserve to die."

"Does Roberti know you are here?" the shifter spat at me, disgust clear in the garbled words he pushed through his growing canines.

The second the chain hit the floor with a clunk, the pain from all the cuts and bruises fell over me as if they'd all just been inflicted. My poor abused body sagged slightly, my knees wobbling on my high heels, and of course that brought a grin to the asshole's face. Even the sword seemed too heavy, and I had to tighten my grip so it didn't fall at my feet. Fen yelped from the hallway, and I prayed he stayed there in case more hunters came down here.

"Roberti who?" Cocking my head to the side, I did my best to smirk at the fool but I was pretty sure I just looked constipated. Everything hurt. "You mean the little bitch that hides behind brainless drones? That Roberti?"

"I'll enjoy killing you." The smile blooming on his distorted face would be one more thing to add to my nightmares.

"Less talking, more killing, shall we?" My attempt at waving the sword at him was pathetic at best.

I walked toward him like a ninety year old grandma suffering from osteoporosis. How did humans live like this? Lost in that thought, I didn't see it coming until the woman screamed. My head hit something hard and excruciating pain exploded in my skull. My weapon clattered on the tiles, rolling away from my noodle-like fingers. *This is what you get for sticking your nose where it doesn't belong*, I told myself as I lifted my body on shaking hands and knees. I was air born again when a kick to my stomach put me right next to the woman and child. She even tried to shield me along with her boy.

I wanted to laugh.

"Keep the boy safe." I groaned and sat up. "My life is not worth your worry."

The asshole cracked a rib or something, but the pain was enough to bring my senses back online. There was always time to lick my wounded ego later, but right then, I had to teach the shifter a lesson. One he would take with him to hell or wherever he was going when I was done with him. Summoning all I had left in me, I stood just as he came within reach, his meaty arms held to the sides of his half-transformed body. Roberti really did a number on these idiots, making them into a mockery of what they were supposed to be. Black veins bulged under his skin, pulsing and fanning out.

"You are one ugly motherfucker," I told him just as he swung for my head again.

Ducking under his flying fist, I took advantage of his strength, twisting myself around him like a snake. My thighs wrapped around his torso, the thin heels of my boots sinking deep between his ribs. I headbutted him and stars burst in front of my own eyes before we both dropped like rocks on the floor. His pained roar rattled the tipped-over table in the corner, as well as the metal bed that had been pushed to the side when I entered. Not wanting to leave things to chance, my hands found his neck and I squeezed for all I was worth. I didn't let go even after I felt his breathing stop.

I couldn't.

"I think he is dead," the woman murmured from over my shoulder. "Are you okay?"

This time I did laugh.

A crazed, high pitched sound before I toppled to the side, twisting my knee awkwardly since my heels were still embedded in the shifter. My breathing was shallow and all I wanted to do was sleep, which was a death sentence inside a hunter's compound if I'd ever seen one. It might not be a bad way to go. Doing so much for someone else should count as a good deed, right? Maybe it would wash away a smidgen of my guilt.

A girl could hope.

"How can I help you?" The woman's face popped above me, her worried gaze wide and frantic.

I knew she was thinking of herself and the two children, that she saw a savior in me when there was none, and she wasn't really worried about my well-being even though I took it as such. I was as pathetic as her at that point.

"The chain," I gasped, barely managing to point to it since it was sitting so close to the door.

She surprised me when she scrambled up, took hold of my limp arm, and dragged me like a mop over the floor to it. I would have never guessed she was that strong. I might be petite, but I wasn't human. We weighed a hell of a lot more than one might think. After placing the chain in my palm and curling my fingers around it, she rushed back to grab the boy. A second later she was kneeling by my side while she clutched the child to her chest.

"My daughter." The words were choked up.

"She is fine," I murmured, closing my eyes to allow the connection to attach again. "My hou—my dog is protecting her."

"We need to run." Hearing the girl was safe gave her new strength. I wished I could say the same. "We have to leave before they come back."

Right, she hadn't seen the art I left in the hallway. I was hoping she didn't faint when we left the room. There was no way I could carry her, not when I wasn't even sure I could carry myself. My eyes were drifting closed, but she shook my shoulder and they opened to her frowning worriedly at my face.

"Right, we need to leave." Flipping over took more out of me than I expected, so I had to take a moment to just breathe, my head hanging low on my shoulders.

"And go where?" The woman crushed the boy to her chest. "They took us from our home. They know where we live."

Turning my head to tell her I'd take them with me, I was startled when I locked eyes with the boy. His mismatched gaze, one blue eye and one green, was curiously searching my face, not an ounce of fear in it. The child was not human at all.

"He is a half blood." It wasn't an accusation, but she jerked away glaring at me.

"There is nothing wrong with him."

"I didn't say there was." Having some of my strength back, I climbed to my feet with my eyes still on the boy. "I should've known that was why you were here."

"He is just a boy." She stood up too, her hackles rising as if she was a shifter.

"You humans should keep your legs closed when you come across a supernatural." That was the wrong thing to say.

"He is a good man," she snarled, and spittle flew from her mouth. It made me smile.

"A male." At her confusion, I blew out a breath and rolled my shoulders. "He is a male, not a man. That's what your people don't understand." When her mouth opened, to argue no doubt, I waved her away. "I'm not one to judge. I don't care if you decide to sprout horns. I do, however, want to get out of here. We can talk about the difference later."

Both of us limped out of the room. Fen glared at me with glowing eyes as soon as I stepped out, but I ignored him. He had to follow me in case there were hunters at the top level. I was not in the position to fight. Picking up the little girl, I had to grind my teeth so I didn't whimper. It'd take time for me to stop feeling the pain and I didn't want to freak the human out more than she had already been. With Fen leading the way, we were almost at the top level when she spoke from behind me.

"Where will we go?"

"I'm taking you with me." Bringing a woman and two children to my home and into my life was a very bad idea. Like, major stupidity, but I was going for it anyway.

"Thank you." She blew out a long, shaky breath, and I felt like she punched me in the gut.

What are you doing, Myst? I asked in my head, and I kept asking myself that all the way home.

Chapter Four

We stood in the middle of my living room staring at each other in silence. The woman with the children hugging her legs, one on each side, while her hands absently smoothed their unruly hair on one side, and me across from her with Fen at my feet and the mother of all headaches pounding on my temples. At least I had the presence of mind to grab my clothing before we left the damn building. The poison the hunters used to coat their weapons had made me sluggish, but unlike any other supernatural, it'd burn itself out in my veins like it never existed.

A perk of being an unknown, I guessed.

"It's worth it." The woman spoke softly, her bottom lip trembling.

"What's worth it?" I frowned at her, wondering if she had a concussion or something because what she said had made no sense.

"Your life." Her shoulders squared up when I stiffened. "Back in that hell hole, you told me it wasn't worth my worry. I'm telling you it is. You saved our lives." A tear left a trail down her dirty face.

"Don't make me out to be some hero that I'm not. I had selfish reasons for what I did. It was just an opportunity to kill more of them, nothing else. You"—I twirled my hand in their general direction—"just happened to be there. That's all."

"If you say so." A small smile played on her split lip.

I didn't do this shit, this mushy stuff with "thank you's" and gratitude. It made me want to puke.

"There is a bathroom down the hall." There was no reason to snap at her but I did anyway. "Go wash your mutts and yourself. I'll leave clothing in the spare bedroom. You'll use it until we find you a place to go."

She took a breath as if gearing up to argue, a glint like fire entering her focused eyes, but then the air around us charged with power and my hand shot out to stop whatever she was about to say as Fen started growling deep in his chest. The woman cowered, pulling the two brats closer to her body. I was only paying half attention to her, my head coked to the side as I waited to pinpoint what I'd be dealing with now. Like I didn't have enough shit already. This was what happened when you tried to do something good. No good deed went unpunished.

"Bedroom. Now," I hissed at the woman, and she didn't wait to be told twice.

The door clicked shut down the hall a moment later.

"I guess the night is not over yet, Fen." The hound snarled at the name, which made my lips twitch.

I lost the smile when I finally understood who was lurking in my home. Anger burst through me like a volcano going off. Pushing past Fen, who was still at my feet, I stomped to the front door and yanked it open, almost ripping it off the hinges. It put me face to face, well more face to chest, with the one person I never wanted to see again in my life, even if I lived ten thousand years. Cold, emotionless eyes scanned me from head to toe before I had time to blink. How the hell did he do that, pissing me off without saying a word?

"Look what the cat dragged in." With a cocked hip, I glared at Fenrir. "Whatever it is you want; the answer is no." I closed the door in his face.

"Open the door."

"Go away."

"If you don't open the door, I'll break it."

"I can always kill you to make up for it."

"You can try." I was either still lightheaded from being slapped around by that shifter earlier or there was amusement in his voice.

"Go the fuck away, Fenrir." His power started pulsing through the closed door, prickling my skin. The idiot was seriously thinking of breaking his way in. I yanked it open again seething. "What?"

"We need to talk." He left me gaping at his back when he shouldered his way in as if he owned the place. "You have humans here." The fae stopped in his tracks, turning in a slow circle like he was expecting humans to jump at him from somewhere. "And shifters." His too-pretty face twisted in a grimace when he sniffed the air, the platinum hair his illusion gave him sliding over his shoulders.

"None of your business. What do you want. Speak, or get the hell out."

"The compound I was going to search for clues on how to track Roberti was wide open and littered with body parts." Those too-blue eyes flashed with something I refused to name. "You wouldn't happen to know anything about it, would you?"

"I couldn't care less about you, Roberti, or anyone else for that matter. I'm a free girl now that Alexius is dead. Your shitstorm does not concern me."

"You know you are covered in blood from head to toe, right?"

"It's a new thing I'm trying. Like a face mask, you know? It does wonders for your complexion, you should try it. Now get the fuck out of my house." I jiggled the door in case he didn't know which exit to take.

"And your hound is bathed in blood, too." As if that was a compliment, the damn hound preened, going so far to even yelp in excitement.

"It's his playtime." Snatching the first thing I could reach, my car keys, I tossed them over Fenrir's shoulder. "Go fetch, Fen."

Both the Fae and the hound narrowed their eyes on my grinning face.

"Using my name, even shortened, for your hound is childish ... even for you."

The black pants he wore didn't hide his powerful thighs when he took a stubborn stance, his feet shoulder-width apart and his arms crossed over his broad chest, which stretched the black long sleeved t-shirt he had on within an inch of its life. The emblem of the Academy over his left pectoral emblazoned in gold was mocking me, so my rational brain took a hike.

"Me? Childish?" I barked out a humorless laugh in his face. "Look at yourself, Fenrir. You use illusion to hide yourself, and that makes a mockery of what you are. And for what?" He stiffened, and I knew I should stop but that ship had sailed the moment he stepped foot in my home.

"Tell me something." Internally I was screaming at myself to shut up, but it had been a long day, so my brain and my mouth had cut ties a while ago. "How does it feel to watch Francesca swoon over Zoltan, huh? Does it rub you wrong to see them together, or when her whole face lights up as soon as he walks into a room? Tell me!" Screaming at him, I took a step forward with my fists clenched at my sides. "Does it hurt? I hope it rips you apart inside. Now get the fuck out of my house."

"You never let me explain, Myst. It's my duty …"

"Get out!" My body vibrated from the rage swirling through me, making my sword materialize in my hand. Even the hound inched away from me as he eyed me warily.

Fenrir stood emotionless, staring at me with an unreadable expression for long enough I thought I'd have to physically throw him out the door. The only reason I didn't say another word was the lump tightening my throat, and I just couldn't push it down enough to speak. No amount of swallowing would shove that bitter pill away. I trusted him once. He cured me of that insanity the moment he jumped at the first opportunity to accept a duty to bond with another female. Too bad she wanted nothing to do with him. Karma was a bitch, but only if you were.

"This is not over." He finally spoke, his deep voice thrumming through my chest.

"It was over a long time ago." I stabbed a finger at the opened door.

"I'll be back tomorrow when you can see reason." Fenrir walked past me, his head held high. "And don't think you'll dodge me, Myst. I've had enough of this."

"Whatever." He wasn't through the threshold yet when I grabbed the door so I could slam it behind him.

"Enjoy your new neighbor." The asshole chuckled. "I heard he is a really nice guy."

I didn't slam the door.

Numbness crawled from my toes all the way to the crown of my head as I watched him saunter from my front yard across the street, open the door to the house there, and turn around to face me. A cocky grin was plastered on his face as he flicked two fingers off his forehead in a mocking salute, closing the door. The doorframe rattled when I slammed mine before pressing my forehead on it.

"This cannot be fucking happening." A treacherous tear trickled down my face, my chest tightening painfully and preventing me from taking a full breath.

Fen whined, but it was just a faraway sound muffled by the whooshing in my ears. Not expecting it, I was startled when a tiny hand wrapped around mine. Turning my head slightly to the side, I looked down at the upturned, snot-smudged face of the little girl, who was watching me with an all-knowing look that didn't belong on a child's face.

"My mommy says I have to be nice, but I will bite him next time he comes."

I barked out a half laugh/half sob, squeezing her hand gently.

"I think I'll bite him too, little brat."

Chapter Five

I desperately needed proper sleep. After the Fenrir fiasco last night, I left the woman and her brats to fend for themselves and crashed hard. The problem with that was I woke up more tired than before I went to bed. All the anxiety about what I would find out when I met with the mage, coupled with the nightmares that had been my companions for as long as I could remember, left me brain dead on the best of days. Not the mental state one wanted to be in when bumping uglies with all the creatures who roamed the night. If my instincts were not on auto pilot, I'd have been dead many times by now.

Stumbling out of my bedroom with my hair sticking out in all directions and half of it plastered on the side of my face, I followed the hushed voices to the kitchen, stopping dead in my tracks when the smell of food hit my nose. With one eye opened, I watched the blurry figures whisper between themselves as plates were being passed over the kitchen counter. It took a good amount of blinking to bring everything into focus, and when the woman smiled at me over her shoulder from next to the stove, I frowned. Something sizzled in a pan she had clutched in her hand, grease spitting everywhere.

"Good morning." Chirping happily, she turned back to whatever it was she was making.

"There is nothing good about mornings," I grumbled groggily, leaning a shoulder on the wall and yanking the hair away from my face. "Unless you are a demon, in which case I might have to kill you."

Silence fell over us all and I glanced at the wide-eyed brats. Scrubbing a hand over my face, I couldn't help groaning. Me and my big mouth. In my defense, I wasn't used to little humans being around me, half-bloods or not. Personally, I disliked younglings no matter the species. Too much noise and too much walking on eggshells around them. Not for the first time, I wondered what had possessed me to drag them to my home. Lapse of judgment would be the end of me one of these days.

"Myst is just like daddy, she needs her coffee before we can see that pretty smile." The woman chuckled, rushing to save my foot-in-the-mouth moment. I didn't miss the scowl she sent my way. "Let's fix her one, shall we?"

The brats scrambled off the chairs and ran around the counter to help her do just that. With a sigh, I trotted to the furthest one from them and plopped down, my eyes watching every move they made. They felt too comfortable in my kitchen. It rubbed me wrong for some reason.

"Since you mentioned it." I wasn't in the mood for talking yet, but I needed to clear the air about few things. "Where is their daddy?"

"My name is—"

"I don't want to know your name." Her mouth closed in a thin line when I snapped at her, but the last thing I wanted was to get more tangled in her shit. The names I already knew were enough to give me enough sleepless nights for a millennium.

"Very well." With her back turned and shoulders stiff, she clanked around the kitchen until she brought a steaming cup of coffee to me, plonking the mug under my nose none too gently. Hot liquid sloshed over the rim and splattered the cracked marble. "They took him before coming back for my boy."

"They? As in the hunters?"

"The ones dressed in white with their faces hidden, yes." Whatever she remembered made her shiver, which in turn raised the short hairs on my arms.

"And instead of taking the brats and hiding, you stayed there waiting for them?" I spat, lifting the burning mug and hissing from the fire licking my fingertips, which made the brats snicker like hyenas. "Cover your ears." Snapping at them made both giggle, their eyes glistening from humorous tears.

"You haven't been around children much I take it?" the woman snatched both brats by their t-shirts—my t-shirts now that I was more awake and could see better—wrestling both wiggling things back into their chairs. "Or people in general judging by your attitude."

"This attitude saved all your lives last night." Gingerly sipping the scalding coffee, which she made to punish me I had no doubt, I watched her through the rim of my cup with narrowed eyes. "Which reminds me. You need to find a place to go."

"I have nowhere else to hide, and they are still searching for us." My teeth were clenched, while her eyes darted all over the place so that she was not looking at me. "I won't give you my name or ask any questions, I swear. Just let us stay here until it's safe to go home."

"This is not a safe house. Too many people already know about it." Another lapse of judgment on my part by allowing Francesca Drake to stay here with that damn shifter Tenebris. Half of the Daywalkers knew where my home was by now.

As if to prove my point, the front door jerked open and Fenrir waltzed inside my house like he owned the place. He stopped dead in his tracks a few feet from the door, cocking an eyebrow in question in a too-familiar, arrogant display. It was enough to give me heartburn. The boy growled deep in his little chest, sprouting fur that stuck out through the collar of his t-shirt, his tiny fingers curling with vicious looking claws. Fenrir's arrogant façade cracked for a moment, interest sparkling in his blue eyes before he wiped it off his face. Because I was glued to the chair, I was too slow to react on the intrusion, and when I glanced at the woman expecting fear or panic, I was surprised to see defiance in her jutted chin. She shrugged at me like she was saying, "The boy is a shifter, so whoever this is asked for it."

"I see you continue collecting strays." Fenrir's long legs ate up the space in three long strides that placed him too close to me for comfort.

"What can I say, I'm a lifeaterian?" It was too early for me to attempt to kick his ass out. "And they can hear you, you know. They are not deaf."

"A what now?" The way he leaned forward made his rain and forest scent fill my nostrils and scramble my brain. Damn stupid Fae.

"Lifeaterian, like a humanitarian only in this case I collect strays." He was watching me incredulously, debating if I'd lost my mind. Get in line buddy. "Why are you here, Fenrir?"

"I thought you'd be more inclined to talk this morning."

"You thought wrong. Now get out."

He opened his mouth but left it gaping when a rancid, acidic scent hit my face like a punch. My head snapped to the side where the boy was last standing, his old t-shirt and shorts crumpled in a pile on the floor. Very slowly, my eyes traveled to Fenrir's feet. A young pup the size of a Pomeranian was tilted to the side on three legs, his fourth, hind leg in the air as he peed for all he was worth all over Fenrir's boot and pants. I tried and miserably failed at keeping a straight face. Fenrir's deep, pained groan only made me laugh harder, tears trickling down my cheeks that I couldn't stop even if I wanted to.

"Oh, this made all the shit I'm dealing with when it comes to you worth it." Gasping, I continued laughing in his face. "Don't you dare touch him."

Fenrir paused half crouched towards the pup as his gaze narrowed at me. Without a conscious thought, I was poised to strike at any moment, all my attention centered on his hands. Fae like him could manipulate reality, but their strongest weapons were their hands. With a twirl of a finger or a flick of his wrist, Fenrir could rip the lifeforce out of a mortal without breaking a sweat. Staying locked in a staring match with me, he squatted all the way down on the balls of his feet.

The pup bared his teeth at him.

"Why do you mark me young wolf?" After a long moment, Fenrir turned to the pup. "I am no threat to you."

I wasn't sure what surprised me more, the fact that Fenrir was watching the pup affectionately, or that the woman, who was waving a scalpel and protecting her child with her body yesterday, was standing unfazed as she watched one of the most dangerous predators trying to scratch the boy under his chin. In the end, it was neither. It was the little girl.

"You have pretty hair." The young child inched closer to Fenrir, tentatively reaching her small fingers towards the platinum strands hanging over his shoulders.

"You think so?" Flashing her a grin, he tilted his head so she could touch him. My ovaries exploded and I had to clench my fists so I didn't punch him. The jerk knew exactly what he was doing, the master manipulator that he was. "Is it okay?" He glanced at the woman, making her blush like a schoolgirl with a crush while she nodded her head a little too enthusiastically.

I glared at Fenrir.

"Take your children in the bedroom." My harsh words snapped her out of her lustful thoughts and propelled her into action.

With a confused look plastered on her face, she snatched the pup up along with the girl, and darted down the hallway locking the door of the bedroom behind her. Fenrir was still crouched in front of me, while I was still coiled in preparation to snap his neck. We stayed like that, the tension between us thick enough to suck all the oxygen from the room. He was the first to break our stare.

"I have a proposition for you."

"I'm not interested."

"I'll make sure the human and her children are safe if you work with me."

My molars groaned from the force with which I grinded my teeth.

"I don't care what they do from now on." If the human saying was true, my pants would've been on fire at that moment. Fenrir gave me a knowing look that called me a liar as well.

There was seriously something wrong with me. I didn't care about others ... ever. I was perfectly happy being selfish. It kept me alive.

"You are still poking at Roberti's operations. This house will not be safe for you, little less them, soon enough." He kept pushing, taking advantage of his sales pitch. "I'll take them into hiding and no one will know where they are. They'll live without you, but I'll make sure you are always there when they need you. You have my word."

"Your word means nothing, which we both know." He flinched at that, and it made me feel better. It was petty, but I didn't care.

"Should I ask Zoltan or Leo to come make a promise?" The hurt in his voice shouldn't have bothered me.

"Ask Leo to come." I made a decision at that moment that would probably bite me in the ass. "Now, or I don't want to see you ever again."

The lukewarm coffee tasted too bitter on my tongue while Fenrir made his calls. Staring at the fridge so I didn't have to look at him, I sipped the brew while my mind raced. I couldn't play babysitter to humans *and* half-bloods. The nightmares were getting too frequent, and they grew worse every time I put my head on the pillow. Something was coming for me, and the fewer people around me when it found me the better. Not for me. I had every intention to go down swinging if it came to that. I just didn't want to add more guilt from innocent lives lost to my conscience.

"Leo will pick them up in an hour," Fenrir said from across the room.

"Good." Placing the mug on the counter, I turned to face him finally. "After they are gone, you have exactly ten minutes to tell me what you need from me. I'll help you, but I'll work alone."

His stiff nod did not convince me that he agreed with the terms.

I should've known better than to trust the Fae.

Chapter Six

"They'll be safe in Sienna."

I had a lot of things to say to Fenrir about that, but I kept my mouth shut because my throat was tight, though the little girl turned and waved happily at me before all of them disappeared through the portal. Leo, true to his word, came within the hour and whisked them out of my house and my life. I should be happy. Damn it. I was happy the brats were out of my hands. The back of my throat tickled. I must have a dog hair stuck in there or something. Maybe I was even allergic to the hound. I tugged on my sleeve in frustration, pulling it down enough to cover my leather bracelet.

"Yeah. Whatever." With the portal closing, darkness ascended around us. It took effort not to shuffle my feet when I folded my arms and turned to face Fenrir. "Out with it. Let's hear what you want."

"You never said where you found the woman and her —" Fenrir started, and as usual, he was off topic.

"That's her story to tell if she feels inclined to share, not mine." When his lips formed a thin white line, I almost smiled. "What do you want Fenrir?"

"If I ask you to hear me out about what happened ..." he trailed off and searched my face. My stomach did gymnastics, flopping around before dropping to my feet. "Would you?"

"No."

"Very well." With a sigh, he yanked on the elastic holding his hair at the back of his head, retying it. The muscles of his arms bulged through the tight shirt he was wearing so much that I had to shake my head to clear it. I wanted to slap him. "A lot of things happened in Sienna. The Order has new members, the old ones took a vacation ... of the permanent kind."

I stayed silent, waiting, but this information gave me a whole bunch of new shit to consider. Could this be connected to my nightmares getting worse? Or the urgency thrumming through my veins warning me that some bad crap was about to go down? He waited as well, expecting me to ask questions, but after a while he cleared his throat and continued.

"There are still moles between us. Roberti knows by now about everything that changed, and it's not in anyone's best interest to wait for him to make his move. While they are figuring out how to get the Academy, and Soren, under control, I need to find Andrius. Many will die if we are not one step ahead of him at this point."

"Soren is awake?" Despite my desire to appear uninterested, the rise in my voice and my eyebrows climbing to my forehead gave away my excitement.

"Unfortunately." Fenrir's face twisted in a grimace. "However, he is the least of my worries right now. Zoltan has that under control ... as much as he possibly can. I need to know Roberti's whereabouts."

"Look at the two of you tangoing like lovers." At his scowl, I grinned in his face. "A perfect tag-team if I've ever seen one."

"Can you cut the snark for a moment?"

"Why would I when it's so much fun to antagonize you?"

"Myst ..."

"Okay, fine. What do you need me to do? Just find which hole Roberti is hiding in? And we are done?"

"Yes." It took him too long to answer, but my feet were moving before his voice faded.

"Consider it done." When the crunch of gravel behind me announced that he'd followed at my heels, I stopped and whirled around. "Get off my ass, Fenrir. I'll find the information and you'll be the first to know as soon as I sniff him out. Until then, I don't want you anywhere near me."

"He is preparing for war, female, so don't be stupid. You can't prance in there alone. You'll need back up."

"Did you just call me stupid after coming to me for help?"

"I need your help, Myst. I don't want you dead."

"Aww ..."

His entire body stiffened when I stepped close enough to him that my chest brushed his. Well it brushed just above his abs since my head only reached his shoulder. When I looked up, the intensity of his gaze nearly buckled my knees, but just as I knew he would, his shoulders hunched and he bent down to come face to face with me. My fingers trailed across his jaw as they used to, eliciting a low growl from his throat. Goosebumps popped out on the skin of his neck when I lifted on my toes, my lips brushing the shell of his ear.

"You worry about me, Fenrir. That's so sweet." A thick arm wrapped around my waist and lifted me slightly off the ground. I could feel his heart beating like a drum in his chest. "But you forget that I cannot die." His arm tightened around me in a painful grip. "Or you would've killed me a long time ago. Now, get the fuck out of my face."

Both of us stumbled back when I shoved him away from me.

Spinning on my heel, I walked away and left him standing with his fists clenched at his sides. His eyes scorched my shoulder blades until I finally took the first turn that took me out of his sight. He wasn't far off when he called me stupid. Lack of proper sleep made me act like an idiot. And in my world, idiots died a painful death. Snatching the phone out of my back pocket, I pressed the only person I had on speed dial. First, I needed to look into my own mess before playing a sniffing dog for Fenrir.

He answered on the second ring.

"Myst." His deep, curt voice cut through my ear drum.

"General, we need to meet."

"Two calls in as many days." If he was mocking me, I couldn't tell. "Does this have something to do with our last conversation?"

"There is a change in the plan." It rubbed me wrong to let people in, but if anyone could help get Fenrir away from me as soon as possible, it was the General. "You want to know what I know."

"Tomorrow, twenty-one hundred hours, same place." He cut off the call.

I stood in the shadows of an ally for a long moment and stared at the phone in my hand until the light of the screen winked out. Was it a good decision to get the human involved in this mess? No. Did I have much choice if I wanted to deal with whatever was hunting me on my own without an audience? Also, no. Humans died every day. Their lives were just a blink of an eye to those of us lurking in the night. It's what I kept telling myself so I didn't dwell on things for too long. With a sigh, I shoved the phone in my back pocket and glanced up at the sky. Even in the darkness, I could see thick clouds gathering as if preparing to unleash a fresh torrent of rain on the steaming asphalt.

"What's with the freaking rain these days?" Huffing under my breath, I stepped out of the alley, blending in with the humans hunched over their phones.

Before I realized where I was going, I was pushing through the doors of the dingy pub. The stale stench of beer and sweat assaulted my nostrils, bringing with it the elusive quiet inside my head. For the first time after leaving this place I could take a full breath. But still, I wondered why this place offered a reprieve to all my troubles. Sliding into the corner bar stool, my gaze locked on the bartender. A nod of his head was enough for my shoulders to drop, then I leaned on the scratched wood of the bar while looking around the place. The plonking of a glass next to me turned me to the human who was watching me warily. The rum and coke was placed on top of a white napkin that absorbed the droplets of condensation trickling down it.

"No trouble." The human grunted, his hands shaking where he was strangling the life out of the towel.

"Nope, no trouble from me." I offered him a smile that didn't reach my eyes.

"That's what you said last time," he grumbled as he walked away.

When he turned his back and no one else was looking

my way, I lifted the chilled glass and rolled it over my forehead. My mind might be quiet in this pub, but nothing could snuff the uneasiness coursing through my blood. It set my teeth on the edge. I'd never felt like prey before and it was messing with my head. I was always the hunter, ready to take a life before anyone knew death was coming. So what, or better yet *who* was after me that triggered all the alarms in my body. I was the boogeymen in this city who had supernaturals scurrying away like cockroaches.

Little did I know, there were scarier things than me moving to town.

Chapter Seven

I felt the air crackle with menace the second I stepped foot outside the pub a few hours later. As much as I liked to pretend I didn't need help, fear clawed at my insides until I found myself running my fingers over the leather bracelet on my wrist. It thrummed on my skin in answer, feeding off my feelings and waiting to be released with anticipation.

"Not yet," I mumbled under my breath just as the first drop of rain splattered the tip of my nose.

Flicking the collar of my jacket up, each of my steps were slow and measured as I tucked my hands in my pockets, the heels of my boots breaking the silence with each click on the pavement. In the early hours of the night, when most humans were blissfully asleep and unaware that their lives hung in the hands of creatures like me, it wasn't unusual to feel different powers mixing with the oppressing air of the city. Yet, this *was* different. It didn't feel right.

It didn't belong.

It was stupid of me to leave the car near the portal, but whenever Fenrir was around, I ended up doing idiotic things. He just had that effect on me, and earlier that night my need to leave him behind had outweighed my concern about where I parked my vehicle. A tremor like ghostly claws raked my spine and forced my feet to falter. The scrape of my metal high heel against the concrete made me flinch and curse up a storm as I tilted my foot up to see if I broke it.

I didn't.

I did, however, almost break a rib when something slammed into me and tackled me to the ground. The heavy body rolled with me until both of us hit the wall of the nearest building. Sharp claws sunk in my side, shredding my leather jacket and my skin, the blinding pain making dark spots dance behind my closed eyelids. The scent of charcoal and burnt flesh made me gag as I curled into a ball under the asshole tucking my knees to his chest. With everything in me, I kicked out and sent him flying off me, which gave me just enough time to groan and press a hand to the gushing wound before I heard him hit the ground. Instead of sounding pained or angered, whoever it was chuckled, and that really pissed me off.

"Feisty." The asshole sneered as I scrambled to my feet, yanking on my bracelet.

A thick chain coiled next to me, the thick fog pulsing before forming into the hound. I swayed on my feet, catching myself with a hand on the wall when I listed to the side. The wound started healing immediately, and it burned like a bitch. My eyes watered, partly from the pain and partly from the odor coming from the creature. Fen snarled and lowered his head, inching his body in front of me to protect me. The hound didn't like me at all. Most of the time, I got the feeling it'd rather rip my throat out instead of save me, but every time I found myself in a shitstorm, he always protected me with his life. I guessed it was a love and hate relationship, which was very similar to all the others in my life.

The creature across from me rolled, but I wished it had stayed down. As he climbed to his feet, my head tilted up until a kink developed from craning it. Easily seven feet, it towered over me from quite a few feet away. Fen's snarling turned feral as thick saliva dripped from his sharp canines, and the creature glanced at my hound in surprise before giving me an appeasing once over. I said creature because I'd never seen anything like him in my life.

With the body of a large, muscled male, he was intimidating enough without the second set of thick arms jutting out of his torso. His upper body was bare, his caramel, sun-kissed skin swirling with red glowing glyphs resembling lava one might see through cracks in the earth. Half-broken black claws adorned his fingers, his fists clenching and unclenching repeatedly. Luckily, he was wearing pants, thought they strained at his groin, which told me he was a little too happy about our collision from a moment ago. Bile burned the back of my throat. His bare feet were actually hooves, matching the two long horns protruding from each temple and giving him the appearance of a bull. None of it scared me.

Not as much as his face.

Shadows blurred his features, twisting and swirling fast enough to make my head spin. Through it all, glowing amber eyes burned too bright from behind the darkness piercing me all the way to my soul. I felt the tug at the center of my chest, the same pull I got when I released Fen from the bracelet. A quick dart of my eyes confirmed no one else was around. I was pretty sure I couldn't handle one of these creatures, so the last thing I needed was more of them.

"It is only I," the creature thundered as if it was offended by my carefulness.

"Oh, look Fen," I chirped, unable to help myself. "Shakespeare got out of his grave to pay us a visit." Even my hound turned to give me a glare at those words.

I grinned at him like a fool.

"So"—Swinging my arm front and back to assure my wound was closed and I could actually move, I took hold of the hilt of my sword with my other hand, making the chain clink together like chiming bells—"how do you want to die?" The words were accompanied by the singing of my blade leaving its sheath. "The easy way? Or the messy, screaming way?"

"It is not I that is needed to die, oighre air a 'chathair rìoghail." The ground under my feet trembled from his deep voice.

The creature lowered his head like a bull and charged me. I was so shocked it called me the heir to the throne that I barely missed being impaled on his damn horns. At the last second, I danced away, spinning sideways from his body and coiling the metal chain around his feet. Fen jumped to the opposite side as if anticipating my move, then together we yanked with all our might. I was lifted a foot off the ground when the creature faceplanted, his momentum making him slide a few feet over the sidewalk before stopping when his head hit the lamp post. I'd bet my sword that if it wasn't for the shadows hiding his features, his face would've been scraped to shit from that fall.

"What did you call me?" I held the tip of my sword pointed at his prone form, which was still sprawled on the ground. "You have things mixed up, buddy. I am a nobody. Definitely not an heir to anything."

The hound grumbled something that suspiciously sounded like he was calling me an idiot, but I ignored him. Supernatural or not, he was a dog. What did he know about anything, besides pooping and eating of course. I jumped back when the creature roared and shifted to his knees. He punched the concrete, and it cracked open as if a meteor had hit the ground. Then, he turned his head and glared at me over his shoulder. The glyphs on his body pulsed brighter when he climbed to his feet. Everything in me was screaming that I should run, but I never listened to that inner voice and I had no intention of starting now. Planting my feet firmly beneath me, I braced for an attack.

It never came.

"Donn Cúalinge, what brings you to the human realm." Fenrir stepped into the light of the now-crooked lamp post.

"This does not concern you, rìoghail an unseelie." The bull creature snarled, spittle flying through the shadows covering his face as if calling Fenrir a royal of the dark court left a bad taste in his mouth. For some reason, I felt the need to defend Fenrir.

"It's a concussion." When both of the males looked at me like I'd sprouted a second head, I bristled. "He is spitting titles left and right like a king throwing gold coins at kneeling peasants." Waving at sword at the creature, I lifted an eyebrow when he glared at me. "He nailed his head pretty bad on the lamp post."

The creature took a step towards me but stopped in his tracks. A freezing wind blasted the empty street, frosting the breath in front of my face. Fenrir moved further into the light, dropping his illusion. Black-as-midnight hair replaced his platinum strands, pale skin stretching over cheekbones as sharp as my blade. His black eyes with white pupils pinned me in place, cutting off everything I wanted to say, like how I didn't need him fighting my battles for example.

Under his illusion, Fenrir was a sight to be seen.

But Fenrir in all his natural glory was simply breathtaking.

The monster inside me purred at the darkness wafting off him in waves. It scratched and clawed to be released so it could join him. It craved blood and violence, and the way Fenrir was at that moment promised that and more. It took a long moment to wrestle it down. The hound bumped his head on my side, snapping me out of the pull.

"You will not be taking anyone's life tonight." Fenrir's voice changed tone, whispering over my skin like a seductive song, and I knew I'd do anything if he only asked. When I had goaded him to be himself, I forgot the power of the voices the Dark Court Fae possessed. I'd be rethinking my choices in the future.

The bull creature swayed, shaking his horned head.

"You will go to your master and tell them that if they want her life, they'll have to go through me first." Another step placed Fenrir between me and the creature.

"I shall tell her, rìoghail an unseelie," the creature grumbled, his thundering voice drowsy as if drunk.

Having Fenrir turn his back on me was enough to wake me from the influence of his words. Anger boiled in my chest that he felt it was his place to get involved in things that had nothing to do with him. As the creature turned to leave with his hooves scraping the pavement, I dashed from behind the annoying Fae and raised my sword over my head, slashing it down and cutting off the creature's head. It dropped on the sidewalk with a wet sound, the shadows disappearing to reveal a grotesque face with pure white, unseeing eyes. The body hit a second later, spraying blood all over my pants. Some of the droplets were sprinkled over Fenrir's pale skin and across his high cheekbones.

"He will not die.' Pinching the bridge of his nose as if I was giving him a headache, he closed his eyes shaking his head. "Not unless his head is attached when you rip out his heart."

"Now you tell me these things?"

"I wasn't aware Faerie was up in arms looking for you, Myst. Anything you'd like to share?"

"I'm a hot piece of ass and everyone wants me?" He glowered when I smiled tightly at him. "No? Not buying it?"

"Why was the bull of Dannu trying to kill you?"

"How should I know, Fenrir?" Snapping at him, I found my sword very fascinating. "Maybe he doesn't like chicks with swords." Shrugging a shoulder, I started cleaning the blade on the dead creature.

"If you don't share what you know with me, I can't help you." I wished he would yell or growl, anything other than the affection he had swirling in his words. "I can't keep you safe."

"You are under the illusion that I want your help. Go crawl into the hole where you came from. I'm doing just fine on my own."

"He will be back." The blood curdled in my veins hearing that.

"I'll lop off his head again if that's the case." Sheathing my sword, I tugged the hound with me down the street not daring to look at Fenrir, although his gaze burned my skin wherever it touched it. "Mind your own business."

"You are my business." Fates help me, but I believed him.

Chapter Eight

Not remembering your past had its perks.

Without being weighed down by whatever had shaped you to be the person you were by that point; you could reinvent yourself. Granted, in my case, I chose to be a killer that did what she needed to do and moved on, but when the predatory instincts were strong, it wasn't like I have many options.

No one could escape their nature.

Circling around the city with the hound drifting in and out of sight, I was lost in thought until I ended up standing in front of the gates of Forest Lawn cemetery. The tall metal gates loomed above me, the golden lions holding a crest looking ominous as if they were angry that I dared to set foot in a place where humans mourned the loss of life while I handed it out daily. It wasn't like I hadn't found myself here before, so they knew the drill. It wasn't our first rodeo.

As I wrapped my fingers around the twisted metal curls on the locked gates and hauled myself up, I couldn't stop the shiver crawling over my spine from the encounter with the minotaur and Fenrir. The trepidation that something was coming started just recently, so I wasn't expecting it to hit as fast as it did. Aware that it must have something to do with all the mess Francesca found herself in, as well as Roberti being his usual asshole self, didn't make me feel better. At all.

Flinging my legs over the top, I sailed through the air landing crouched on the other side. The only sound apart from a couple of night birds chirping was the thud of my feet hitting the concrete. The hound shifted into a thick shadow, passing through the gates and materializing next to me with an unimpressed look on his face. Unless we were in a fight, he looked just like a Doberman to anyone who saw him. It was much easier to explain a dog than a hound the size of a pony who loved killing as much as I did. I glanced at him from the corner of my eye, seeing him look around the dark cemetery as if expecting someone to jump us at any moment. He might like killing a little more than me.

My feet were moving, eating up the space through perfectly tailored lawns and rising monuments, the cloudy sky hiding the beauty of the rolling hills and elegant headstones flush to the ground. That was the pull this place had on me. The mixture of traditional and modern coupled with the tranquility caressing my skin. There was still a light drizzle misting through the air, dampening my skin as I strolled further in until I found myself in front of the Gardens of Contemplation.

Ironic, I knew.

I just couldn't resist the 360-degree view of the city, the lights blinking at me and flirting with my senses.

There was beauty in death.

Many might not see it as such as they selfishly cling to

those around them. It might also be a human thing because their lives were so short in comparison to ours, but to creatures like me with no end in sight, it represented bliss. No more endless decades or centuries blending together until you couldn't even remember what year it was. No more moving to change names or identities to escape notice.

Peace.

If that was what I wanted, why was I hell bent on staying alive?

I had no answer to that apart from the feeling inside me that I was meant to do something. The problem was, whatever that thing might be, it had been buried along with my memories. Only the need to survive was left like a burning coal in the pit of my stomach. Speaking of which ...

Slinking into one of the secluded gardens, I curled my legs under me and plopped on the damp grass. Thank the Fates for leather pants. No one wanted wet underwear rubbing tender skin when they walked. Reaching in my pockets, I pulled out one of the coals I always carried on me along with my phone. The hound stood there for a long moment just staring from my face to the rock in my hand before walking to a more interesting view, I guessed. I rolled the coal around my fingers, the rough surface scraping over my skin. With the mist still drizzling, it left black smears on my pale skin, its energy pulsing and playfully teasing mine.

A pouch of these coals was found in my pocket when I was discovered dumped on the Daywalkers' doorstep. They tried to take them, but it zapped anyone who tried to oblivion. The only way they could get their hands on them was if I handed them over freely, and I'd only given two away from the time I woke up that day until now. One was to Francesca Drake, and she returned it after she used it to call my presence without understanding the significance of her act. The other was to Fenrir. Before shit went south and I didn't want to see his face anywhere near me.

He never used it.

Still looking at the coal, I didn't notice that I was pressing the phone, the screen lighting up until the ring echoed in my ear. If I had been in the right state of mind at the time and not so much of an idiot, I never would've pressed the call button. But after the fourth ring, the call was answered and a tense silence stretched uncomfortably from the other side.

"Twice in one day." The General sounded raspy from sleep. "The situation is either very bad, or you are dying." When only the night birds chirping around me were his answer, he became more alert. "Where are you, Myst?"

"Do you ever think about dying, General?"

"Coming from you this could be a treat, but I'll assume you have a different reason for asking," he said on a sigh, which came after a long stretch of silence where the only thing I heard was the rustling of fabric from the shifting bedsheets in the background.

"I shouldn't have called." Pulling the phone away from my ear, I had my thumb poised to end the call.

"Wait!" His shout was muffled through the speaker, and that momentarily froze my actions.

"It's late, you should sleep." A halfhearted statement if I'd ever heard one.

"Since I'm awake now, might as well hear what made you call." A soft chuckle accompanied his words, soothing the uncomfortable feeling pinkening my cheeks from the guilt that I woke him up in the middle of the night. "I can't say it happens often enough. It's not something I want to miss."

"In case you want to hold it against me like a vulnerability?" My barked, humorless laughter echoed around me, bouncing off the trees. "Think again, General. I can snuff your life before you have time to realize you are about to meet your maker."

"All the time." His softly spoken words caught me off guard enough for me to pull the phone away from his ear so I could frown at it.

"What?" My confusion made him chuckle again, the sound relaxing my stiff shoulders.

"I think about dying all the time," he clarified, the clinking of glasses following his words through the speaker of the phone.

I'd watched him enough before I decided to trust him to know that he was pouring himself a glass of scotch, two fingers deep, no ice. It might sound stalkerish but if you lived my life, you'd be careful who you let in as well. Know your enemies, but know your friends better. It was the latter that would stab you in the back when least expected it.

"You are as old as some of these rocks, General." Trying for a lighter tone, I snickered when he grumbled unhappily. "Wouldn't it be freeing if you could just close your eyes and not deal with life and everything it throws at you ever again?"

"I'll have you know that I am in my prime." He huffed jokingly before the sound of his voice shifted to a more serious tone. "You'd think I would be tired of it by now, but I'm not ready to wave the white flag yet." That last part was murmured as if he was lost in thought.

"Why?"

"I beg your pardon?" I almost laughed at his startled question.

"For a human, you are old enough. Why aren't you ready? What makes you keep going when even your body is letting you down at every turn." I could hear his throat working while he took a sip of his drink.

"It might be a human thing," he said, his tone thoughtful. "Life is so short, and before you know it, it slips right through your fingers, leaving so many things you wanted to do behind. If I am honest with you, I've been thinking a lot about what life would be like if I was like you. If I was turned immortal."

"Real life is not a fiction, General. You don't get turned into something like me with a bite. We are born, not made. You know this."

"I might be as old as rocks, but I still understand simple things like that," he said dryly, pulling my lips up in a smile. "The truth is, being immortal is every human's dream. Even when they don't admit to it."

"The grass is always greener on the other side," I mumbled into the phone, turning my attention back to the coal in my hand.

"Have you ever thought about dying?" For the second time, he caught me off guard.

"About myself? Not really, no." I rubbed the back of my hand that was clutching the coal over my forehead. "But so many die and end up under the ground, their names eventually forgotten with time. Did you know that the cemeteries are like gardens?" My eyes stretched over the outlines of the hills. "They are full of fertile soil where each and every one of those dead are planted like a seed. A seed that never sprouts. I wonder if maybe the gravediggers dig the holes so deep to prevent that from happening."

"Why are you thinking about this now?" The General was a very observant man. I forgot that about him.

"There are things more powerful than me out there,

General. I can't always find a way to avoid them, and there comes a time when you have to face what's coming for you."

"Very true," he hummed under his breath. "If I know anything about you, I know that you will go swinging if it ever comes to that. I haven't known you to ever tilt your throat in surrender." I could hear him swallow through the phone for a long moment, as if the conversation made him toss the drink back until he drained the glass. "You are not a woman to go meekly to her death."

"I'm not a woman, General. I am a female, not human."

"I know, Myst." I might've imagined it, but there was tenderness in his words that formed a lump in my throat. "The question is, do you? Because if you know what I do about yourself ... instead of contemplating dying, you should be contemplating killing whoever or whatever comes after you."

"So bloodthirsty for a human." The heat in my words was missing, but I did make him snort.

"I'll have more questions tomorrow night." All humor gone, he was back to business. I loved that about the General.

"I would expect nothing less. I might not give you an answer, but you can always ask."

"Goodnight, Myst." For some reason I didn't end the call straight away. "Do me a favor, would you?"

"And what's that, human?" Calling him human made him laugh.

"Between now and tomorrow night, if anything comes after you"—my fingers tightened around the phone, almost crushing it— "rip the motherfuckers apart."

"I'll try." I couldn't hear my voice from the hammering of my heart buzzing in my ears.

"You better be at the arranged place tomorrow night; you know I hate waiting." He cut off the call.

My fingers tightened over the coal, the hard rock digging into the skin of my palm. The magic from it zinged through my arm, making it tingle all the way to my shoulder. All the scents intensified around me and the darkness of the garden brightened as if coming alive in front of my eyes. Cracking my neck, I rolled my shoulders and stuffed the phone back in my pocket.

"Sir, yes Sir." Giggling, I answered to the night, although the General couldn't hear me.

I could definitely keep myself alive for less than twenty-four hours, right?

Chapter Nine

"Where is your dog?" I groaned when I heard Fenrir at the front door right before it clicked shut.

The Fae was like an ulcer, painful to have around but there was nothing you can do to get rid of it. Apart from it being surgically removed, of course. Closing my eyes, I pictured lopping off his head with my sword and smiled happily at what my imagination created. His boots thumped an even tempo over my floorboards before stopping. Through closed eyelids I couldn't see him, but I felt the heat from his body burning my skin. He was standing too close.

"What are you up to?" When I did look at him, he was squinting at me in suspicion.

"You need to stop coming here uninvited." Leaning with both elbows on my kitchen counter, I blew the steam curling above my cup of hot tea. "You and my dog have something in common apart from the name, of course. You both chase tail. That's where he is at the moment…just like you." The more his pretty face darkened, the bigger my smile was. "Unlike him, you picked the wrong tail."

"You are up to something, Myst. What is it?" Just like the proverbial dog with a bone, he wouldn't let it go.

I sighed.

"Okay, since I can't wish you away, I'll play along." Huffing, I turned around and leaned my back against the counter, crossing the arms over my chest. "What makes you think I'm up to something? It's too early in the morning, even for me, to cook up trouble." Flicking my fingers in air quotes on the word trouble, I watched a muscle twitch at the corner of his left eye.

"You are smiling." Fenrir growled at me like I'd just committed the greatest offense in history.

"I smile plenty, thank you very much—"

"Usually when you smile, someone ends up dead." He spoke over me, his hand slicing in front of him and chopping the air.

"What is your problem, Fenrir?" My frustration was strangled when he took a step closer, boxing me in between his body and the counter, which was digging into my spine.

"My problem is"—Hunching down to put us face to face, his hands anchored on either side of me so I couldn't slide away—"there was a minotaur in the middle of a human city—Donn Cúalinge to be precise—trying to kill you. The bull of Dannu has not been seen in over a century. I need to know why."

"Maybe he was taking a sabbatical and he wanted to make a grand entrance to announce his return?" My attempt at shrugging a shoulder looked like I was spasming, but Fenrir did that to me. He messed with my head. "You'll have to speak to him about his comings and goings, I'm afraid. Oh wait!" Snapping my fingers in his face, I enjoyed his glower. "You can't because I cut his head off. Oops." I shoved him away from me with both hands. "You're welcome."

"He is not dead." Fenrir yanked on the elastic holding his ponytail, angrily collecting his hair to retie it. "Donn Cúalinge is goddess touched. His physical body can die, but that only sends him back to Faerie. Which means he will be back in no time and more pissed off than ever."

Being aware that something was hunting you like an animal was one thing. Knowing what that thing was and that it couldn't die was a whole new level of clusterfuck. The back of my skull went more numb with each word coming out of Fenrir's mouth. The asshole just couldn't have kept that information to himself.

"Why are you bothering me, Fenrir? I thought Roberti was your main concern. Go hassle him, would ya? I'm pretty sure he is putting together a plan for world domination or something. I, on the other hand, am not."

I'd go to my grave without admitting to anyone that I actually squeaked like a teenage human girl when he yanked me to him, his arms tightening around my waist. I couldn't look away when his illusion dropped, leaving me staring at his black eyes with those white pupils that were so intense I had no doubt he could see my deepest, darkest secrets. My body sagged in his embrace, succumbing to his power and scent, which was filling my nostrils and scrambling my brain.

"There are enough in Sienna to deal with Roberti," he murmured under his breath, those all-knowing eyes flicking to my dry lips. "I made many mistakes in my lifetime, Myst. It's in my nature to honor my kind. It's what I was born to do, yet here I am. Scared out of my mind that you will die and I won't be there to protect you." My mouth was left open, the words drying on my tongue when he continued. "Or die beside you trying."

"I don't need your sacrifices, or your protection. I can keep myself alive." A small lie but not in million years would I tell him or anyone else that I needed to be saved. "I had the bull under control. He was sprawled on the ground after kissing the lamp post before you popped up. You just created a distraction for me. That might get me killed."

"Sacrifice was agreeing to do what Soren and my court asked of me as a royal. Following honor bonds for the sake of bloodlines. Being by your side is not." He pressed his forehead on mine, exhaling deeply and closing his eyes. "I beg of you, let me help you. If it's your wish, I shall leave when we have dealt with it and there is no threat to your life. I couldn't bare it knowing you are fighting alone."

Closing the distance between our faces, I pressed my lips to his. My hands were clutching his upper arms and I felt his muscles stiffen like stone under my fingertips. For one long second that lasted an eternity, and not long enough at the same time, my lungs burned from holding my breath. It had been years since I'd felt his mouth on mine, and I'd been unaware of the hunger my body had for him. Ashamed of being an idiot and succumbing to his prowess, I started pulling away.

With a deep groan that sounded like it was coming from the depths of his soul, he jerked me back, painfully tightening his grip on my waist. His tongue aggressively pushed past, parting the seam of my lips, plundering my mouth with such ferocity I felt dizzy in seconds. Fenrir was not kissing me back. He was trying to devour me whole and that would leave a bigger mark than anything he had ever done before.

His mouth and tongue were leaving a brand, and I was powerless to stop it.

You would think the Fates were mocking me when after days of gray clouds and rain, bright sunrays streamed through the open windows to frame Fenrir in a halo of light that contrasted with his dark hair. I clawed at his shoulders, desperate to pull him closer and push him away, my conflicted emotions only adding to the insanity battering the inside of my skull. Fenrir's hand smoothed over my back, stopping on my ass where his fingers tightened before he lifted me off the ground. My legs wrapped around his narrow waist, pressing his erection to my center until I was gasping into his mouth from the electrifying currents shaking me to my core.

He wouldn't let me pull away to take a breath.

His shirt was gone and so was mine while we shared the same air, our lips fused together so intensely it would take one of us dying to separate us. My back hit the kitchen counter a moment before my pants were ripped off my body, followed by the panties and Fenrir's pants. His hands were everywhere, his touch harsh like he was trying to assure himself that I was real by bruising my flesh. I was on fire. Everywhere we touched skin on skin was burning, and I thought this was the way I'd go. It'd be him to turn me to ashes and I'd disintegrate without giving a fight.

A scream was ripped from me when he wedged himself more firmly between my legs, entering me in one powerful thrust until his pelvis hit mine. Stretching me across the counter, he got a white-knuckled hold on the edge with one hand and a bruising grip on my hip with the other. His face was twisted in a snarl that should've scared the shit out of me, his power blasting out of him like an inferno. Instead, I didn't think I'd ever seen him more beautiful.

Every muscle of his body that I could see was outlined from the tense way he held himself. The sun was casting shadows over his pale skin, creating dips and divots I wanted to trace with my tongue but could only trace with my fingers. My channel was burning from the harsh entrance of his cock inside me, spasming around his hardness. Mewling noises were passing through my lips I'd never thought I'd hear from myself. It only drove him wilder. Fenrir roared, baring his teeth at me, and then he began to move.

I was digging my nails into his skin, leaving bloodied lines across his chest and abdomen so I could keep myself from flying off the counter. His hips were pistoning between my thighs, each thrust harder than the one before. All thoughts fled my mind, leaving behind only my need and a lustful, dazed cloud. Somewhere in the back of my mind I screamed that this shouldn't be happening. Nothing should feel this all-consuming and intense, but on the outside, I was giving as good as I got, my body lifting to match his every move. A coil tightened in my lower belly as sensations I couldn't name spread through my limbs.

Then I started to glow.

If Fenrir was as surprised as me, he didn't show it. There was an intense look of concentration on his face and he kept pounding into my body like his life depended on it. I was also way past rational thought, the need to reach the high only he could give me pulling me deeper into the abyss like a siren song. All I knew was the feel of his hands running all over me and the feel of his cock stretching me to a point of pleasure-pain. My skin, on the other hand, had a different plan.

Runes started popping up over my skin, each swirling and curling as if an invisible artist was going to town over me with a brush. The more pleasure I felt, the faster the symbols were spreading, a deep red glow peeking through the split skin. Fenrir sped up his tempo, the soft grunts and growls coming from his chest preventing me from losing my shit over what was happening to me. Like I wasn't spread out under him like a sacrifice lit up resembling a Christmas tree.

"Hold on to me." His words were garbled, so I expected to see fangs growing in his mouth.

There were none.

What I could see was his features sharpening, his high cheekbones that were already sharp getting pointier angles. Same type of runes, although with thinner lines, started appearing over the skin on his face, the red glow matching mine. They rushed from his cheeks down his neck, spreading like veins over his broad shoulders. He kept thrusting with all he was worth, and I kept encouraging him, unable to stop myself. I knew if he moved away I might go crazy and attack him. The coil tightened further inside me. That was when the white iris in Fenrir's eyes started to glow.

The coil snapped, hurling me into such an intense orgasm, I felt I was drifting in endless darkness with no physical body in sight. Somewhere from a great distance I could hear myself scream, and a second later I was yanked back in my body by Fenrir's primal roar that rattled the cupboards in the kitchen. Colors were bursting behind my closed eyelids, my body twitching and quirking in his arms. He didn't let go of me, and he didn't stop moving. I felt like my heart was going to explode. And that was when it happened.

A scorching hot blast of power washed over us both.

My back bowed off the counter, another stronger

orgasm melting my insides. Fenrir arched his back and roared at the ceiling, his body jerking between my thighs out of his control. It lasted an eternity where no mortal or immortal should feel that much pleasure. And then it was gone.

Fenrir slumped over me, his sweat-slicked skin sliding over mine. I expected us to both be burning up, but he was too cold to touch. And so was I, if his hiss before he jumped back was any indication. His hard shaft, still throbbing and pulsing from pleasure, however, stayed firmly inside me. Coming out of the daze, he blinked at me before a line formed between his perfectly shaped eyebrows.

"Are you okay?" His voice was much deeper than I'd ever heard it.

"Mmm hmm …" My lips were tingling, and I was unable to form words for a long time. "What was that?" I finally gasped, filling my lungs with much-needed air.

"I don't know, but we are about to find out if we can experience it again."

I had no time to argue because he started moving again.

I had every intention of kicking his ass after he was done fucking me.

I was smart like that, sometimes.

Chapter Ten

The afternoon sun was warming my skin where I was stretched out on top of Fenrir. He picked me up like a boneless sack and carried me to my bed where he arranged my body over his like a blanket. I had every intention of getting up and moving as soon as my limbs started cooperating enough to obey my commands. A content sigh left Fenrir while his hand glided up and down my back. Thankfully, all the runes on my skin that had made me a glowing freak show were gone. Though a strong urge to ask him if he saw them too gnawed at my stomach, but I didn't want to know that I had imagined it all either. Choosing ignorance as the best option, I closed my eyes and focused on simply breathing.

"Are you ready to share what you've been up to?" Fenrir murmured, his deep voice vibrating through his chest under my cheek.

"You are a good fuck, Fenrir, so let's not spoil it with chatter, huh?" I patted his chest halfheartedly, and he chuckled.

"I'll go along with whatever stops you from running. If you want to use me as a stud, by all means do so." His large hand pushed the hair sticking to my sweat-covered forehead away from my face, and when he tucked his chin down, he peered into my eyes. "Why is a goddess-touched Fae trying to kill you?"

It could've been that I was still basking in the afterglow of all the orgasms he gave me. Or maybe whatever it was that had happened between us had melted my brain, because my mouth opened and words poured out that I never would've told him if I was using the rational part of my brain. Fenrir had broken my trust, yet here I was spilling my guts like some novice. I deserved to die for that alone.

"And the last couple of days, the feeling of urgency and that something was hunting me intensified, making it impossible to sleep without feeling like I'm drowning," I finished spilling my secrets. "The nightmares are bad enough that it takes me a good five, ten minutes just to catch my breath when I wake up. Always the same thing. I stand in darkness and can't see anyone around me, but I can hear their screams." His arms tightened around me when I shivered involuntarily.

"Shouts and weapons being drawn are singing through the air while my heart is hammering so fast and so hard that I'm pressing both hands to the center of my chest to stop it from breaking my ribcage. There is a voice whispering from behind me, saying, *'You have to run where no one knows who you are. You must forget until it's time.'* It's always followed by a splitting headache that causes the eyes to roll to the back of my head. Just before I wake up, all sounds stop. The screams, the shouts, the clinking of metal. The silence is choking me, shriveling my lungs while my mouth opens in a silent scream. The voice whispers again, only this time from inside my head, *'You must forget until it's time.'* Then I wake up coughing and gasping for air, the stench of burning coals searing my nostrils."

I was squirming uncomfortably on top of Fenrir, but for some stupid reason the feel of his skin on mine made it easier to talk. Not looking at him helped, too. This last part was a bit tricky, but I just went with the flow. No one liked a half-assed story anyway. I could always pretend he was making it up if he asked about it again.

"You can't remember any other sound or scent from your dreams?" He kept the even tempo of the strokes on my back. "An energy signature, a power leak? Anything at all?"

"No." With a sigh, I rolled off him and stretched my arms over my head. I was deliciously sore in all the right places. "But that was when I started feeling like someone was watching me. Yesterday was the first time it attacked. And the funny thing is, there is this knowing inside me that the minotaur is not the *IT* I should worry about."

"So what's the plan?" Lifting on his elbow, he leaned over me and searched my face. "I know you well enough to know you are trying to be one step ahead of this. I'm here and I'm not going anywhere, so make peace with that. Might as well use me to help."

"I'm not some damsel, Fenrir. I'm a killer."

"A very pretty one at that. Don't deflect, though." He cupped my face, his thumb rubbing over my cheekbone. "You are hiding something." When I narrowed my eyes at him, he snorted and shook his head, his midnight hair sliding over his shoulder and spilling over my bare chest. "After today, I get glimpses of your emotions. It's something that we will have to talk about in the future, but not now. You are nervous, so I know you are hiding something."

It was a dangerous thing that I liked seeing him in my

bed and didn't feel like ripping his heart out for saying I was nervous. I was, but that was beside the point. Fenrir was more dangerous than whatever was after me.

"I'm going to gain access to my memories." His gaze was too intense, so I turned my head to look out the window, pretending like I couldn't feel his eyes burning a hole in the side of my face. "Living unaware was a good thing while it lasted, Fenrir. I would've left everything as is if I didn't know I was about to die." Snorting a humorless laugh, I shrugged a shoulder. "Well, they think I'm about to die. I have no such intentions. I need to know what's after me, why it wants me dead, and then I'll figure out how to kill it."

"You have found a mage with psychic powers." It wasn't a question, so I didn't answer him. "How? The ones slipping through the portal out of Sienna don't last a week before their powers send a flare and someone is dispatched to either drag them back or kill them."

"I hope you don't expect me to answer that."

"Very well." He nodded to himself, which triggered all sorts of alarms in my head. "I suppose I'll just have to wait and see."

"If I need help, you'll be the first I call." I had no intention of doing so but he had no need to know that. "Until then, go chase Roberti. Or I don't know, go play hide and seek with hunters. I've heard it's good exercise to keep you on your toes."

"You can allow me to come with you, or I can follow you." Fenrir gave me an arrogant smile that I was desperately itching to slap off his face. "I'm good with either option."

"My contact might not be happy to see me bringing another person along. I can't risk it." In a last-ditch effort to convince him to leave me be, I smiled at him. Stupid of me, really. Suspicion plastered all over his face in a split second, and I groaned in response. "You can't come Fenrir. Humans get twitchy around us as it is. I need his help. I can't have him going into hiding because you think we are going to play house."

"I can deal with humans; I've learned a trick or two from Zoltan." He lowered his head and started trailing kisses over my body, which scrambled my brain all over again. "He won't even know I'm there."

My fingers tangled into his long, silky strands and I tugged his head up so I could kiss him. The Fae was like a flame and I was a moth. I knew I'd burn if I allowed myself to be close with him, yet my tongue slipped past his lips and I lost myself in his taste. The scent of rain and forests surrounded me, and I kept telling myself this was only a small distraction I'd allow myself for the moment. I might die tomorrow, so at least I'd go without being sexually frustrated. Wherever our souls go after death, I was sure no one wanted a bitch entering that space anyway.

I was becoming a better liar daily, but I was mostly lying to myself.

Chapter Eleven

That's how we found ourselves driving through the streets with Fenrir perched in the passenger seat as if he belonged there. The lights we were passing illuminated his face for a split second before shadows hid him from my view. I was partly paying attention to where I was driving, and partly giving him side-eyed glances as if he would turn around and bite me.

This was a very stupid idea.

I fell asleep for less than an hour after our last session of monkey sex, and for the first time I didn't dream. It must've been because I was tired and well sated. We had an attempt at a relationship before I left Sienna and settled in the human realm. I've slept next to him many nights and I had the same nightmares. This was something new I wasn't willing to examine too closely, so I occupied my thoughts by thinking about the weather, of all things. At least there was no rain today at all.

There was always that.

My foot lifted off the gas pedal, slowing the SUV to a

crawl as we neared the abandoned warehouse. Without taking a turn off the road, I stopped a couple of yards from the entrance and gave Fenrir an expectant look. His head turned slowly as he scanned the area before his gaze settled on me. I cocked an eyebrow that yielded no results. Putting the car in park, I leaned toward him and a slow smile tilted the corners of his lips up, at least until I smiled back and put our noses an inch from each other. His eyes narrowed just as I opened the door at his back, they widened comically when I shoved him out of the car and onto the sidewalk. In a graceful twirl, he managed to stay on his feet, though he stumbled while beautiful cuss words spilled from his lips. I snickered.

"Stay out of sight."

I slammed the car door closed in his face and drove off.

"This is what you get for agreeing to stupid shit," I muttered in frustration. "Damn it, girl, it's like you have never seen a cock in your life."

I have seen enough that if I was human I'd be ashamed to admit the number. But a cock was a cock when you need to scratch an itch, but Fenrir was not just anyone. I should've remembered that before allowing him to get between my legs. Just thinking about it had me squirming in the leather seat.

The abandoned warehouse was just as I left it, standing unassuming in the darkness on the outskirts of the city. My body was jostled when the tires dipped in the potholes on the uneven, narrow road, gravel pinging a staccato under the car. Tightening my grip on the steering wheel, I wrestled the heavy vehicle through the already opened chain of the entrance.

The General was early.

Fenrir's stubbornness might just save my life if this was a

trap, and after my stupid phone call, the human might have decided it would be safer for everyone to get me off the streets. I did sound like a lunatic waking him up to talk about death and graveyards. I'd lock me up in a padded room if I were him too. I knew that he respected me, but it was only because I saved his life on a handful of occasions. I also knew that he was afraid of me, as any mortal should be. My gaze flicked to the rearview mirror but nothing other than dark, empty space was there.

The General was standing in the middle of the open area in front of the warehouse, the yellow lights of my car dancing over his silhouette before I brought the vehicle to a stop. Leaving the engine running, I opened the door and hopped out, sending my senses wide to search for someone that shouldn't be there.

I couldn't even feel Fenrir.

He might've gotten pissed off and left. If this was a trap, it'd serve me right.

"General," I greeted the man watching me with curiosity glinting in his gaze.

"I must say I'm happy to see you in one piece." He cracked a rare smile, the wrinkles around his eyes deepening, and I shuffled my feet before catching myself. This made me understand better what Fenrir felt when he got suspicious of my smile.

"Is that why you are early?" Rolling my shoulders, I dropped the illusion hiding my sword, revealing the hilt where he could see it sticking from my back. "You are never early, General."

"I've actually been here for over an hour." It was his turn to shift uncomfortably, the worry flashing through his face making him look his age for once. "I'm an old man, Myst. With age we get sentimental about things we never considered before." He pursed his lips and gave me a calculating look. "I never know if you will save me or be the end of me, but over the years, I've developed a soft spot for you. It won't sit well with me if you get hurt."

"Aww, you charmer. You like me, admit it."

"As much as a human can like a pet shark without being eaten." His teeth flashed white when he grinned, making me giggle.

"I like being a shark."

"I know." The General chuckled good-naturedly before getting down to business. "You wanted to see me."

"I discovered that the hunters are kidnapping half bloods hiding in this city." A twinge between my shoulder blades made me dart a glance around, but the night was quiet without a peep of sound. "A day after we met, I visited one of their compounds and managed to save a woman with her two children. One of them, the boy, was half shifter/half human."

"There were more in that place?" The ferocity on his face would've made anyone else take a step back. It made me breathe easier knowing that the human cared.

"Just the woman and the two children. I killed everyone else."

"What do you need from me?" When I cocked my head to the side, he snorted. "You didn't call me here to tell me what you could've said over the phone."

"I need all the known buildings searched and preferably the innocents rescued unharmed. Do you think you can do that?"

"What am I looking at?" As I've said many times, the General was a smart man.

"The same thing I saved you from. Skilled killers, faster, stronger, and with no remorse. Bullets won't stop them, they'll just piss them off. You'll need people to go in unnoticed and kill as many of them as you can before anyone is aware of what's happening." And just because I owed him that much, I tugged gently on the bracelet on my wrist and swallowed thickly. "I'll give you help, but I can't be a part of it."

"You'll be busy with my mage." He nodded courtly.

"He is not your mage, General." I liked the human, but I didn't like him that much. "You will do this for me?"

"I will do it for me." Folding his hands at the small of his back, he watched me for a long moment. "What am I to do with those that will be rescued. I assume you have a plan in place?"

"The truth is, General, that I might not live to see your success." He was frowning at me but I appreciated the fact that he didn't cut me off. "I would like to think you would take care of them and keep them safe. The hunters will meet their end soon enough, and you might help speed up the process with this mission. I came to you because I don't think those half bloods have the time to wait. Do this, and consider your debt to me paid in full."

"You are a good person."

"Don't confuse me for something I'm not, General. This is for selfish purposes only. I hate those assholes and will never pass a chance to make their lives hell. Plus, you'll keep them busy and out of my way. That's all there is to it."

"I'll agree under one condition."

"There is always a catch with you, huh?" Snorting, I waved my hand in his face to hurry it up so he could spill his request. The twinge was stronger this time, burning a hole between my shoulder blades. I had half a mind to tell Fenrir to stop glaring at me.

The General snatched me by the arm, startling the crap

out of me enough to pull me behind him. His broad shoulders hunched as he reached the waistband on his back, pulling out a mean-looking gun. The point of the barrel waved left and right as he scanned the darkness for threats. Shaking off the surprise at his reaction, I placed a hand at the middle of his back to calm him down, not wanting the human to get trigger happy and fill Fenrir with bullets like a pincushion. One of the General's hands was still holding onto my upper arm as he used his body to protect me.

Silly human.

"Unhand her at once, human." Fenrir's snarl curdled my blood. His voice came from behind us instead of the empty space facing us.

Yanking my arm free, I spun around the General pulling my sword out at the same time. Keeping the tip pointed to the ground, I tugged on the bracelet, not caring who saw my hound for what he was. The shadow pulsed and thickened, and he materialized next to me already hunched and baring his teeth at the darkness.

"Fenrir, protect the General. I need him alive." When he just grumbled like a spoiled child, I finally snapped. "You said you want to help and for me to trust you. Here is your chance to prove your words are not just empty promises."

I felt him coming close as he placed himself between me and the General, the human gasping something that sounded like a prayer to his God. One quick glance over my shoulder explained why. Fenrir dropped his illusion, and on top of all his dark, menacing glory, his runes swirled and glowed on his face and neck. He resembled a deity if I'd ever seen one.

"What are you?" The General finally gathered his bearings and cleared his throat.

"An asshole," I answered for Fenrir with a snicker. "But

this is an asshole that can keep you alive to keep your word."

"She is always this charming," Fenrir drawled, making the General bark his laughter.

"Yes." The human chuckled, regaining his grip on the gun that was dangling from his fingers. "Yes she is."

Oh, goody. They were bonding. How nice.

That was when the minotaur stepped out from the darkness, twice as large as I remembered him. And this time he brought friends.

Chapter Twelve

"What the fuck is that?"

The General snapped loud enough for only us to hear him, his energy signature flaring up and teasing my senses. Not for the first time I wondered if he was something other than a human. In my peripheral vision, I noticed Fenrir stiffening and turning to appraise the old man with renewed interest. That was not good.

"A cow." Raising my voice loud enough to be heard by our attackers, I grinned when the minotaur snarled. Fenrir choked on air. "It used to be a bull, but they chopped off his balls. Now he is a cow looking for them. Isn't that right sweetheart?"

I'd been aware that my mouth-to-brain connection didn't always function as it should. Blurting offensive things had always been my go-to in any situation, but I also knew that one day it might cost me my life. Like today, for example. The minotaur hunched his shoulders, lowered his head until his glare was at eye level with me, and then he charged.

"Fenrir, the General." Hissing my order, I raised the sword and braced to intercept the creature.

Behind the fast-approaching horns that were overtaking my vision, three ghouls were spreading around to try to box us in. The ground under my feet was quaking with each stomp of the hooves, which were the size of my head I might add. I could hear Fenrir murmuring something, but I couldn't pay attention to what he was saying. There was a five-hundred-pound bull headed my way who was adamant about impaling me on one of the protrusions sticking out of his temples.

A gunshot rang through the air.

I swayed on my high heels and listed to the side when I lost hearing in my right ear. Smoke puffed out next to my head and I managed to uncross my eyes long enough to see the General lower his gun slightly. His face was grim, and his mouth was pressed in a firm line. That was when I noticed the ground stopped shaking. My head jerked to the side and a snort escaped me when I saw the minotaur's confused face as he reached up to touch the hole between his eyebrows, which was trickling blood down his nose. He brought his fingers in front of his face and rubbed the blood between them, then his eyes snapped up to zoom in on the human.

"Great." I couldn't hear myself talk so I was probably shouting like an idiot. "Now you just pissed him off more." For the first time since I'd known him, the General took a step back.

"What in all the Heavens is that?" he repeated his question from earlier. That was when his head swiveled and he saw the ghouls. "Myst? I need a weapon. Now!" the General barked, the command in his voice snapping my spine straight.

Dropping his gun, he turned around, placing himself back to back with me. Fenrir joined on the other side, and my hound positioned himself to next to my thigh to complete our half-assed defense against four almost unbeatable creatures. Swishing the sword through the air, I slightly bent my knees. I'd had worse odds.

"I only have the sword. Fenrir can let you borrow one of his." I was watching the minotaur, who'd changed his tactics and was circling us like the predator that he was. I moved with him, forcing Fenrir and the General to do the same. "I'll take the cow, the two of you keep the ghouls busy so they don't interfere ... and make sure you don't die."

"I will not babysit the human when you need help." Fenrir sniffed like the arrogant ass that he was.

"First, you assume I'll *need* help." The minotaur was smirking as if he knew something I didn't. The hound snarled like a feral beast, shaking his head and spraying thick saliva everywhere. "Second, the human will protect the half bloods he will save from the hunters. Didn't you ask for help? That is sure to cause enough ruckus to keep Roberti's attention on other things so you can deal with him."

"You really have lost your mind." I bumped into Fenrir when he stopped moving. "You got humans involved with Roberti?"

"He is not just human, Fenrir. You can't tell me you didn't feel his flare up earlier." I shoved him to get him moving before I lost my visual on the minotaur.

"What?" the General stuttered, stumbling and messing up our attempt at circling the enemy for the second time.

"Never mind."

"Nothing ..."

Fenrir and I spoke at the same time, which only made

the human growl in frustration. Fenrir shoved a vicious-looking dagger in his hand, I assumed to sidetrack him or get him to shut him up. It worked. With a tight grip on his weapon, the General resumed his watchful guard.

"I'll pull the cow away from the two of you, just stay alive until I can join you," I mumbled to Fenrir.

"You need to stop calling the goddess touched a cow," Fenrir reprimanded, but I was already moving.

As soon as I separated from the two of them, the minotaur charged again. He looked more menacing with the blood drying on his face, but unfortunately, the bullet hole was already closed. He was much closer this time around, so he reached me in no time. Spinning around, I danced away from the horn as thick as my thigh, slashing with the sword in an arch. The blade sliced through the creature's neck and shoulder, sending a spray of blood in the air.

The cut was not deep enough.

He skidded to a stop and turned to face me with a freaky-as-hell smile on his lips when I gawked at the fast-healing cut on his body. His skin was as smooth as a newborn's, but before I could register what was happening, he was charging me again. The chain from my wrist wiggled and a black blur hit him out of nowhere, tackling him to the ground. When they stopped rolling, I saw the hound with his jaw clamped around the minotaur's neck as he shook his head for all he was worth. With a sweep of a hand, the creature sent my hound sailing through the air.

"Fen!" My ribs tightened painfully when I saw him hit the ground and bounce a few feet. Luckily, he wasn't far enough to restrict me with the chain.

"I'm fine," Fenrir called from my right, which pissed me off.

"Not you," I snapped, stomping towards the bull that

was still on his knees. "Don't you ever"—Jumping in the air, I spun around, kicking out and catching him in the head so hard his neck snapped back and he toppled over—"touch my hound again, you fucker!"

Moving faster than I expected, the minotaur was on his feet, his meaty hand wrapped around my neck. Lifting me off the ground like a doll, he chuckled gleefully, his fingers tightening until dark spots started dancing at the corners of my eyes. I clawed at his wrist with one hand, not willing to release my sword. I just needed to be a little closer to nail him with my weapon before I passed out. To my horror, the minotaur reached with his other hand and started yanking on the chain connecting me to the hound. Panic worse than his hand around my throat shriveled my lungs.

"You will never live to take your place, *oighre air a 'chathair rìoghail*," the creature hissed, his putrid breath melting the eyebrows off my face. I gagged, my vision tunneling. I could hear Fenrir shouting something in the background, but I couldn't understand what. I just hoped he kept his word and protected the human. "Look at you, *gun chuideachadh*," the minotaur spat in disgust.

"What?"

Gasping like a fish out of water, I was weakly kicking my legs hoping he would relax for a second before I couldn't save myself. He watched me warily, so with great reluctance I uncurled my fingers and dropped the sword. It hit the ground below me with a thud, and the idiot grinned.

"I said helpless." He was gloating as he brought me closer to his face. The cow must've eaten shit for breakfast, lunch, and dinner. I was ready to vomit all over him. "She was right when she said you were unfit to rule. A human has more power than you."

"Who is she?" Rasping, I hung limp from his hand. Just an inch closer, that was all I needed.

"Your sister, of course." Everything in my head screeched to a halt, leaving white noise buzzing between my ears. "Oh, I see you didn't know." The shit eater chortled. "Dannu herself raised her. She is the one befitting the crown."

"What ... what crown?" My arms and legs were numbing, and the lack of oxygen was muddling my brain. The cow was talking shit out of his ass, because if he was looking for a royal of the Seelie or the Unseelie, he needed to go after Fenrir or those like him, not me.

"The Courtless throne will rise again. All will kneel before it."

He was so passionate about it, his eyes filled with a manic glint as he shook me like a rag doll. That brought me as close as I needed to be. Wrapping both hands around his wrist, I swung my lower body like a pendulum, flipping it up and twisting my legs around his arm. With a surprised shout, he stumbled backwards, but I was already kicking back and piercing his shoulder with the thin heel of my boot. He roared, his fingers loosening around my throat. Wrenching his digits back until I heard them crunch, I lifted myself just as he started lowering his arm. Reaching over my head, I grabbed hold of his horns and flipped over to straddle his shoulders. With quick work, I wrapped the chain around his neck and dropped behind him, tugging on the metal with everything in me. Like a cut-down tree he went down, clouds of smoke wafting up when he hit the hard, packed dirt.

Still gripping the metal tight, I cocked my hand back and bent over him, punching him with all my strength in the chest. Fenrir said to kill him I had to rip his heart out while his head was still attached. That was exactly what I was planning to do.

The crunching of bone was like music to my ears, at least until the pain made me see stars. I was biting the inside of my mouth so I didn't scream like a little girl when my whole fist shuttered. The minotaur released a pained grunt because I punched the air out of his lungs, but his heart was still very much operational under his ribs.

"Myst?" Fenrir huffed as he came up beside me, the General following right behind him. My eyes flicked towards my nose so I was seeing four of them. I giggled like an idiot.

"You lied!" I coughed, sputtered, then started biting my tongue just to redirect the pain.

"I beg your pardon?" Even with his hair sticking out all over the place and dirt covering him from head to toe, Fenrir managed to look down his nose at me.

"Rip his heart out you said," I whisper-screamed at him, grinding my teeth.

"That's the only way to kill him." Fenrir looked offended while I wrestled with the chain one-handed to keep the minotaur down. The General's eyes were as wide as saucers, as if he was watching an exciting tennis match.

"Have you done it?"

"Well, no." A line formed that puckered his eyebrows, and I had to mesh my lips together not to scream. "I've never had a reason to wish to kill him ... until now."

My hand was already mending so the broken bones snapping back in place was worse than the original shattering. Acid burned the back of my throat as I swallowed the rising bile. Keeping my mouth shut so I didn't hurl, I jerked my chin towards the sword to show the General I was in need of his assistance. It took him a moment, but he eventually snatched it and handed it to me hilt first.

"Take hold of the chain Fenrir, don't stand there like a lump."

"I was waiting for you to ask or you'd bite my head off," he muttered angrily under his breath, and he almost lifted the barely-conscious minotaur off the ground with the strength of his tug.

Going for the sword with my good hand, I nearly toppled over the cow when the chain cut my reach short. Turning a death glare on Fenrir, I lengthened the chain at my side slowly while daring him to say a word. His right eyebrow crawled up his forehead as he did the same to me. Without breaking our staring match, I grabbed the sword and stabbed the minotaur through his chest so hard the tip of my weapon imbedded in the packed dirt deep enough to pin him like a bug for a science project. And just because Fenrir pissed me off, I twisted the sword for a good twenty seconds, keeping eye contact the whole time.

"We dispatched the others." The General cleared his throat.

"At least you are good at something apart from spreading false information," I told Fenrir before walking away to check on the hound.

Dropping on my knees, I ran my hands over his body, noticing the bones that were healing under his hot-to-the-touch fur. The horse hairs rasped on my palms and he whimpered weakly. He was alive and that was all that mattered to me. As soon as I pulled him back in the bracelet, he would be as good as new.

"The human killed one of the ghouls. I killed the rest." Fenrir loomed over me, his shadow hiding the lights from my car. I might need a new battery for the SUV since it had been running all this time.

"How?" Not that I wasn't happy that the General could look after himself, but I would find it trying to kill a ghoul without my strength or durability.

"It would appear that your human has a berserker gene in his veins." My ass dropped on the ground and I craned my neck to gape at them. Shit just couldn't get much worse for me right now.

Chapter Thirteen

"Oh, shit." The words were a breath passing my lips.

"I've never searched for bears." The General sounded like we'd just insulted him.

"Easy there, human." Lifting both hands palms up, Fenrir tried to calm him down. That was when I noticed the General's shirt and jacket hanging in tatters on his shoulders. "We are not talking about animals."

"What is going on here?" The human turned on me, his face darkening in anger as his shoulders grew before my eyes. "What were those things, Myst? This is my world and I need to know what we are up against so I can protect it. Don't make an enemy out of me."

"He needs to calm down." Fenrir spoke loud enough for only me to hear, but the General narrowed his eyes at him.

"You have no reason not to trust me." Scrambling to my feet, I faced the human. The incredulous look on his face called me a liar. "Yet. Not to trust me, yet," I amended to placate him.

"You yourself told me not to trust you." He brought up a good point. Me and my big mouth.

"You shouldn't on many things, but for this you'll have to take a leap." Turning to Fenrir, I said the words I never thought I would. "We need to hide and come up with a plan. If what you said is true, when the cow shows up again, he will be much stronger, and I doubt he will only bring a handful of ghouls with him next time."

"I know a place." It was the General that offered, surprising me. I thought his rage was too strong for him to have a rational thought. "You wanted a meeting with my mage anyway," he added when I was quiet for too long.

Fenrir stiffened, his eyes alert and his features tight, fully tuned in on the conversation after the words he just heard.

"Don't even think about it, Fenrir. Here is your chance. You want to follow the Daywalkers agenda? If that's the case, get the fuck out of my face or I will kill you." Rubbing the bracelet on my wrist, I tugged on it twice and the hound faded into a shadow that pulsed two times before being sucked into it, chain and all. "If you want to stick around, keep your mouth shut and stop plotting. It's unbecoming, even from you."

I walked away from both of them so I could pick up my sword. A twinge shot up the back of my hand all the way to my elbow when I took hold of the hilt with both hands. The broken hand might be healed, but it'd hurt for a while. Putting my back into it, I yanked my weapon out of the dirt, sinking the heels of my boots an inch in the process. With a huff, I jerked those out too, most probably looking ridiculous.

"I'll keep the two separated." Fenrir followed behind like a bad smell I couldn't shake. "But you have a lot of questions to answer first."

"I wouldn't think you'd do anything without gaining something in return, Fae." Flashing him a grim smile, I peered around him at the General. "Where do we meet you?"

"We go together, or it's a no go." The human had every right to be suspicious, but I was not in the mood for it.

"We will still know the place, you know that, right?" I ignored Fenrir's penetrating stare, keeping my eyes firmly on the human. "There will be nothing to stop us from coming back if we choose to do so."

"I can move the safe house. If I'm with you, you can't arrange a raid on the place tonight."

"You think we need more than just the two of us?" Snorting, I shook my head at his logic.

"For where I'm taking you?" the smile the General gave me sent a shiver up my spine. "Yes, you do."

"Very well." Twirling my hand and regretting it when pain rolled my eyes to the back of my head, I clenched my jaw and pulverized my molars. "Hop in, your Uber has arrived for pick up."

Not waiting for any of them, I stomped to the SUV, yanked the door open—using my good hand this time because I was a quick learner—and jumped in. Fenrir's voice drifted to my ears as he murmured, "Uber?" to the General, and the human answered by saying, "You are not from around here, are you?" A moment later they both climbed in the car rocking the vehicle with their weight, Fenrir riding shotgun and the General arranging his limbs in the back like he was a president going for a drive. The Fae was still minus his illusion, all dark haired and otherworldly with his faded runes sill glowing slightly on his face. I tried but failed to hold back my laugh.

"What gave him away, General?" Locking eyes with the

human through the rearview mirror, I kicked the car in reverse and pressed the gas to the floor. "Was it his attitude, or his accent that told you he wasn't from around here?"

The General glared.

A sound like the popping of blanks being shot, turned my attention to the body of the minotaur, and my eyes widened dramatically, just like Fenrir's. The creature's head exploded like a melon. We looked at each other before twisting around to see the General frowning.

"We need to work on the delay. It's too long," he muttered more to himself than to us. The human was more resourceful than I gave him credit for. I'd have to ask him about the bullets at a later time.

I shouldn't have antagonized him, especially when I still needed his help, but men, or *males*, were so easy to rile up. I simply couldn't resist the chance whenever it presented itself ... like now. Only silence answered me, so I swiveled around executing a perfect turn to point the nose of the SUV at the road, and then I used my lead foot to get us out of the warehouse with billows of dust and gravel left in our wake. Keeping it quiet, however, was wishful thinking.

"You have a hound by the Courtless throne." Fenrir's warily spoken words had my hands tightening on the steering wheel, and me grinding my teeth through the pain in my hand. He pursed his lips and I braced myself. "It would make sense if ..." He shook his head like he was trying to stop himself from blabbering. "It can't be. There must be another explanation."

I opened my mouth, but no words were coming out. They died on my tongue when he reached in his pocket and pulled out the coal rock I'd given him what felt like another lifetime ago. He rolled it between his fingers, his eyebrows puckered in thought. The gasp coming from the General had my head jerking straight, and I yanked on the steering wheel to level the car, just missing a parked vehicle by a hairsbreadth.

"Good, you are paying attention instead of sleeping back there." I grinned at the human; like me nearly crashing the car had been a planned maneuver.

"You two might be immortal, but some of us in the car can die from a crash." He barked at me.

My grin grew just like his glower.

I wish Fenrir glowered, too.

No, his gaze was still pinned on my hound and the coal in his hand.

"What did the Donn Cúalinge say to you, Myst?" I squirmed in my seat like my ass was on fire, though I said nothing. "The goddess touched," he prodded after a second, as if I was deaf and not ignoring him on purpose. "What did he say?"

"I don't know." Shrugging nonchalantly, I kept my eyes on the road. "He was spitting all sorts of nonsense, and I was trying to kill him and stay alive. I didn't pay attention."

Fenrir didn't believe a word I said, and I didn't care.

"Which way, General?" A change of subject was in order and getting the human to play GPS was as perfect as any.

The Fae stayed silent, giving me side-eyed glances while the General turned me around ten times through the same roads until finally deciding to give me the right destination. I was at the end of my rope in regards to my level of patience, and his explanation that he was trying to make sure we were not followed didn't help any. We were predators, every single one of us. We didn't need to follow a car, we just used our noses and instincts to find a trail. Try explaining that to a human that was a second away from activating dormant genes and going all hulk in your car. Yeah, no. I kinda liked the SUV. So, I sucked it up, probably cracked a tooth or two from grinding, but I kept my mouth shut and sat there staring through the windshield at the white picket fence, the nicely-trimmed lawn, and the light blue house with a porch. A rocking chair was placed next to a side table that had a potted fern in it, the wide green leaves bowing over the ceramic protecting its roots.

The General cleared his throat in question.

"It looks"—I blinked at it stupidly—"very human." At Fenrir's snort, I pressed my lips together firmly so I didn't swear at him. "Very domestic," I amended like that made it better, then I stared at the Fae from the corner of my eye.

Fenrir chuckled.

"You really don't value your life, do you?" Snarling at him, I hopped out of the car so I didn't kill him for real.

"It has to be unassuming. The better it blends in, the less anyone will pay attention to the comings and goings." The General sounded proud of himself when they joined me outside, and I begrudgingly agreed with him.

"You will bring the mage here?" Hating the fact that they could hear the nervousness in my voice, I plowed through. "Might as well get it over and done with while we make a plan to deal with the cow."

"You really need to stop calling him a cow," Fenrir mumbled. I ignored him.

"Let's get inside before we attract attention." The human looked pointedly at Fenrir. "You are sure he is safe to be allowed inside?" That question was for me, so I tilted my head and pretended to think about it.

Fenrir narrowed his eyes, a muscle jumping on one side of his jaw.

"I can always kill him for you, General." Eventually

Fenrir and I were going to really kill each other, or at least end up in bed again. The tension between us was making even the General squirm.

"I'll hold you to that," the human chirped too cheerfully. "Wait." His hand wrapped around my arm and he held me back when I tried to move.

With both eyebrows raised, I watched him pull out his phone and press a button, his hold on me never ceasing. Fenrir's eyes zeroed in on the General's hand, his white iris flashing in anger. A flick of my hand stopped him from divorcing the human from one of his limbs.

"General, we have a visual on both subjects accompanying you. We wait on your signal." A disembodied voice came through the speaker of the phone. Even Fenrir looked impressed.

"Stand down, these are friends"—The human gave me a shrewd look before speaking again—"this time. If you see them again without me, shoot to kill."

My nod of agreement had him releasing my arm, and I realized it had all been planned. He hadn't been just trying to manhandle me. By physically holding me back, he was not just using words to tell his soldiers that we weren't a threat, he was also showing them with actions. My respect for him went up a notch, and Fenrir bowed his head in acknowledgment, even though it was barely a tilt of his chin. It must've hurt him a lot to do it, too.

Without further delay, I bolted down the short path and up the two wooden stairs to the porch. Grabbing the metal door handle, I was twisting it just as the General called out a bit too late, because I already had the door open a bit.

"Myst, no!" the human shouted just as a blast of magic punched me in the boob and shoulder, pirouetting me off the porch and faceplanting me in the neatly-trimmed grass.

Chapter Fourteen

Shouts were accompanied by the crashing of a door into something, then there was a lot of snarling. The buzzing in my ears quieted as I flopped on my back, groaning and spitting a mouthful off grass. Thankfully, the cow was sent in time out, or I didn't think the minotaur would let me forget this moment for as long as we tango.

"Fenrir." I rasped, lifting on both elbows but barely able to hold my head up. That mage packed a good punch.

"I will put a bullet in your head if you try to get past me again," the General snarled, pointing a mean-looking gun with a very long barrel at Fenrir's nose with a surprisingly steady hand.

I said surprisingly because the look on the Fae royal's face would be enough to make a supernatural tuck tail and run. The runes were pulsing and glowing red on his face and neck, an invisible breeze swirling the hair around his head. This time his eyes, iris and pupil, glowed to bathe the General's face in the light while casting shadows.

Fenrir looked magnificent.

"Fenrir!" I snapped louder, regretting it the same second when my head felt like it was about to explode.

My body was lifted off the ground, making me gasp and clutch Fenrir's shoulders to stop the vertigo. I didn't even see him move. If all these were perks from our sex session, I needed to talk to a manager. A refund was in order since I got none of it for myself. If I remembered it correctly—and I did; I really, really, did—I participated as much as he did.

"It's my fault." It was obvious I couldn't talk without groaning or moaning. "I should've known the mage was already here. I didn't think."

"I will melt the skin off his bones and force him to eat it." He was holding me a tad too tight, but I didn't think it was the right time to tell him that.

"Aww, look at you going all caveman about little 'ol me." At last, he started glowering at me, so I attempted a smirk. When his pissed-off features shifted into concern, I decided to abandon trying, a sigh leaving my lips. "I need the mage alive ... for now."

As much as I was being delusional and pretending I was some rebel saving creatures left and right, I'd always been about self-preservation first. The General might have a soft spot for me, but he was aware of that little fact, too. Hence, why he was always careful when we met. We could all play friends and allies as long as it never came between us. It might not be right, but I would never regret staying alive. My words calmed Fenrir down as well. I guess he knew me well, too.

"Put me down; I can walk." Slapping his face none too gently and then pretending to pet him earned me another glare. At least he didn't look worried anymore.

With Fenrir's help, teetering precariously on my high heels and hanging on his arm, I walked up the porch for the second time, smiling at the General. "He is getting stronger."

"He has enough time to practice being locked up here." The gun didn't lower, so I placed my hand on the barrel and pushed it down.

"Fenrir reacted however he reacted to protect me. You can't possibly hold that against him." There was still resistance on the gun, and I knew if I moved my hand it'd come up. "He also protected you tonight, General."

"Not a hair goes missing on the mage," he spat, but at least he put the gun away. Small victories. I also elbowed Fenrir to snap him out of it because his power was searing my skin.

The General stepped away, and I walked in the house passing the tilted front door hanging on the bottom hinge alone. There was a hole in the middle of it that I guessed Fenrir must've punched into it while I was too busy eating grass. Splinters of the wood were sprayed in the entrance as I gingerly stepped around them, discovering a spacious living room to my right. A male sat on a two-seat sofa with elbows braced on his knees while he held his head between his palms by fistfuls of hair. His face jerked up just as I entered.

"Myst." The mage jumped to his feet and braced himself.

"What? You think I'll attack you?" Snickering, I ignored the way he cautiously sidestepped around the sofa to place it between us and plopped on the closest armchair with a groan, closing my eyes. "Relax. My head is still swimming from your tantrum. I need to rest before I do anything else."

Silence was my answer, so I forced one eye open to see him googly eyed and pale as a ghost staring at the front door. Rolling my head on the chair, I saw Fenrir looming there and blocking the General from coming inside. Males. It was all a dick measuring contest with them.

"Fenrir, either walk in or get out. We don't have time for your shit." Turning to the mage, I stabbed a finger at the sofa across from me. "You, sit."

"What is your name?" Leave it to Fenrir to start with pleasantries even while he is pissed off.

"No names," I snapped a little too harshly. The mage jumped and darted behind the sofa again.

"His name is Marius and he has been living in this city for the last fifteen years before he came across Myst." The General knew I didn't want to know names, so he'd given it on purpose. It was his way of giving the mage, I guessed Marius now, an additional layer of protection. I only knew a handful of names of the ones I'd killed.

"Well played." I bared my teeth at him. His lips twitched in a barely-there smile.

"Myst might not kill those she knows by name." Fenrir stepped next to my chair, folding his arms across his chest. "But I don't have those issues."

"Yes Fenrir, we know you are death incarnate, watch us all tremble in terror and wet our panties," I drawled when an idea swiveled my head towards the General. "Do you wear panties, General?" His face paled before reddening, and I grinned so big my cheeks hurt. "I would've pegged you as commando but what do you know—"

"I thought you needed his help." The human hitched a thumb at the mage. "I need to make a few phone calls, so I'll leave you to it." He was out of the living room like his ass, covered in panties probably, was on fire.

"I don't know anything." The mage spoke, his sentences coming out in a rush and blurring together. "I haven't left this house since you dropped me at the General's feet. I can't help myself, much less you."

"Calm down." With a tired sigh, I scrubbed a hand over my face flaking off some dried dirt no one told me was there. "I need to remember things that are blocked from my memories." When the mage clamped his mouth shut, I cocked an eyebrow. "You can do that much."

"You will do it now," the caveman next to me ordered, setting my teeth on edge.

"Thank you, Fenrir. You are dismissed; I don't need a narrator."

"I am not leaving." He looked down his nose stubbornly.

"Then shut up."

"I will do it, but only if you bring someone that can erase my memories afterwards." The mage, Marius, grew a pair of balls. "You will kill me otherwise."

I just stared at him with a blank face.

He squirmed, clearing his throat. "You won't kill me because you respect the General, and he is planning to use me unless I know something you don't want anyone to know. Not that I have anyone to tell. You would've killed me by now if that wasn't the case."

"I'll wipe his memories." Fenrir turned out to be the star of the show.

"Is this yet another perk from fucking like rabbits?" I craned my neck to see him better in case he lied. "This shit is getting old. I was a participant, too. Who do I contact to get the nifty tricks I was cheated out of?"

"Zoltan taught me some of his tricks." Fenrir smirked, his eyes burning from the hunger I could see there. Pressing my thighs together, I jolted upright because I didn't want him to see what he was doing to my girly bits.

His arrogant chuckle told me he was well aware.

Asshole.

"I need you to dig through my head," I told Marius, cursing up a storm in my head for starting to use his name. "Either unlock it so I remember everything when I open my eyes, or you better write everything down to a dot. Am I clear?"

"I'll make sure he follows instructions."

"You are not staying Fenrir. Go keep guard at the door or something." Although I was waving him off, he didn't budge.

"Myst," he growled my name like a warning, and I huffed, both hands thrown in the air in my frustration. Marius startled.

"Okay, fine. Why do I give a shit what you hear or think anyway?" Snapping my fingers to get Marius's attention, I pointed at my head. "Open Sesame. Shazam!"

"You give your word that you will erase my memories?" He had a hopeful look as he gazed at Fenrir. It made me want to scratch off his face. I didn't stop to question why I was more than my usual agitated and pissed-off self.

Fenrir offered a regal nod of his head.

A snort escaped me.

"Close your eyes, and no matter what, don't fight my magic." Marius finally stepped in front of me, both of his hands raised palms facing me.

"Here goes nothing," I muttered under my breath before I was plunged into my worst nightmare.

Chapter Fifteen

Black stone encircled me and it went so high I couldn't see the ceiling of the building I found myself in. Flames flickered at even intervals down the long, never-ending room, their flares a deep shade of red that was almost black, too. It was casting a chilling kind of vibe, accompanied by the echo of silence that felt as if I was boxing my ears. It was as beautiful as it was terrifying.

My heart jackhammered in my chest.

Tall, narrow windows stretched on either side of me, the tainted glass etched with intricate markings like swirls dancing over the surface. Silver beams fought to burst through, which only added to the horrific beauty of the place. Fingers itching to take hold of my sword, I turned in place and took it all in. It reminded me of what Death's perfect home should look like, yet it gave me a calm feeling that almost doubled me over when nostalgia hit me like a brick to the back of my head. Somewhere in the back of my mind, I was aware that Marius was poking through my memories and trying to unlock what had been hidden from me a long time ago. Knowing that made my eyes prickle with unshed tears, so I scrubbed the back of my hand over them in frustration.

I didn't cry.

Most definitely not about a stupid room. One that looked like a cliché for some dark lord or something equally nonsensical. It was something Roberti or his cronies would love, I was sure. My eyes drifted to my feet, tracing the blood-red stone with pinprick sparkles through it everywhere the silver beams or flares of flames reached it. The cry of what sounded like some large bird pierced the quiet blanketing me, forcing me to spin around fast and search for it. No furniture was in the room, which left the warning echo bouncing off the walls for a long time before it faded away.

A girl giggled happily, the sound stopping my heart for it to resume hammering my ribs with renewed vigor. Whispers reached my ears that seemed to come from nowhere and everywhere at the same time. The girl giggled again, shrieking in joy and raising the short hairs on the back of my neck. A shiver raked my spine when something brushed my shoulder and arm with a ghostly touch. My skin prickled and anger bubbled in my stomach as I unsheathed my sword, the singing of metal loud in the eerie quiet, but I hoped it would stop whoever was trying to scare me in their tracks.

Silence could be so loud.

As loud as the heartbeat in my ears.

Pale skin with long blonde hair like spun gold broke the unreal view of the room. A girl around seven, maybe eight years of age gingerly crept towards me, her bare toes poking out from under a long, dark gray night shirt with black flowers embroidered in it. She looked like a child, but when she was close enough for me to see her face better, her eyes turned the blood in my veins to ice. An ancient being was peering at me through the young girl's gaze.

"You shouldn't be here." Her head tilted to the side unnaturally like a bird.

"Yeah, no shit."

Blurting things out was definitely my way of escalating a situation from bad to worse in an instant. Pointing my sword at her might not have been too smart either judging by the amusement flickering in her eyes.

"Say…" Changing tactics before shit hit the fan, I tried for curiosity. That works on a child, right? Even a creepy-as-fuck one. "Nice place you have here. Very … grisly. Where is here anyway?"

"Your home, of course." Lifting an arm so skinny I was expecting it to break from the movement, she gestured around the place. "What it used to be before Danu decided she would change destiny."

"This Danu sounds like a real charmer," I drawled, making a grimace that had the child giggling. "I met her cow, twice." The smile disappeared from the girl's face.

"Donn Cúalinge." The girl hissed like a feral cat, flinching back and baring her very sharp, very pointed teeth. "She has finally found you."

"Well, I sent the cow back to her so nothing to worry about." I wasn't sure my nonchalance fooled the child … or maybe being? Creature? Whatever she was, when she straightened, she gave me an annoyed look. "What?"

"I can feel your powers, girl. They are still as locked as they were from the start." While my eyebrows crawled to my hairline, she grinned, her expression stabbing me like an ice pick between my breasts. "If you bested Donn Cúalinge, it's only because they were testing you. You would've proven to be as capable as a lamb headed for slaughter."

"This is bullshit." Pissed that she was insulting me, I glared at her, and that only broadened that messed-up grin of hers. "Isn't this supposed to be my memories? It means either the mage is fucking with my head, or I've finally lost it and I'm making shit up myself."

"Ah, you have sought the truth on your own. This is good. Very good. Perhaps it is time." I frowned at her. Maybe everyone in this place, including myself, was insane. It would explain a lot. "You are smarter than you look," she decided.

"What's that supposed to mean?" Taken aback, I was ready to slap her—whoever she was.

"For a moment there, I thought hiding your memories might've addled your brain. You did not strike me as very smart." She looked so serious I did take a step closer, bringing the tip of my sword to the center of her chest.

"You blocked my memories?"

"Who else has the power to do it if not me?" It was her turn to take offense.

This was ridiculous and I was tired of everything. Rubbing a harsh hand over my face, I let the sword drop down, the tip clinking off the floor. It looked like this was a bust, my memories still hidden from me by some invisible barrier. This creature was too nuts for me to make up, so it might be a failsafe or something. A trap to discourage me, maybe? Whatever it was, I didn't want any part of it.

"Okay, I'm good to wake up now," I shouted to the hidden roof above our heads.

"Who are you talking to?" The girl also craned her neck while squinting toward the ceiling.

"The mage. I don't have time for this." Placing the

sword at my back where it belonged, I slapped both hands on my hips and raised my gaze. "Yo! I need out of here, like now! Or I will kill you."

"You will not leave unless I allow it."

"Fine, I can kill you." Dropping my head to pin her with a glare, my fingers brushed the leather bracelet on my wrist. Something that didn't go unnoticed and even earned me an approving nod. "You never said who you are."

"Exactly."

"Who are you?" I pushed the words through clenched teeth. I was way past annoyed at that point.

"The better question would be ... do you know who you are?"

"I love this game. I'm Myst. A hot chick with a mean sword and a bad attitude. Now your turn."

It happened so fast I had no time to blink, little less attempt to protect myself. What felt like a meteor slammed in my chest and propelled me head-over-heels through the air until my poor body hit one of the far walls with the crunching of bones. I was desperately trying to reach for my hound, but no part of my body could move when it dropped on the blood-red floor, which was still twinkling merrily as if I wasn't about to die here. I was a ball of pain and misery, my face numbing from my shattered cheekbone, which was resting on the cold ground. Apparently, it wasn't enough. My body was flipped over, the girl looming over me before she snatched me by the neck with a surprisingly strong grip. The cow could learn a trick or two from this bitch. My hysterical laughter sounded suspiciously like a pathetic moan.

"You think you are ready to know what I hid from you to protect you, girl?" she snarled, her nose an inch from mine while her face twisted in a horrifying grimace.

Power brushed over my skin, familiar and welcomed. I could feel Fenrir trying to reach me, hopefully, successfully pulling me out of this shit storm. The creature in a girl's body smiled, a chilling tilt of her thin lips before she pushed Fenrir's energy away as if it was nothing. A faint, pissed-off roar could be heard from very far away, and of course that made her chuckle.

"Well aren't you a real surprise." With her free hand, she patted my face, which sent a new wave of agony through me. "You just might be worthy. You might even survive to take your rightful place." Twisting above me, she sat on my chest, though she didn't release the grip on my throat. "If memories are what you want back, who am I to deny you. Watch."

She twirled her hand in front of her, pushing my face to the side in time for me to see swirling shadows condense and start pulsing in the middle of the huge room. My eyes watered when ice-cold wind blasted us from the center of it, before plunging us into a different room.

And a different time.

Chapter Sixteen

If there was one thing good about the situation I found myself in, it was the fact that the pain from my broken body was gone. As a matter of a fact, I wasn't sure I had a body in this place and time, although I still felt the girl holding me by the throat. Weird, and unsettling to be sure.

My attention was pulled to the two large thrones made of dark green stone speckled with black dots and yellow lines twining through it at random places. One was taller than the other, both of them had dark red pillows positioned on the seat. Six large rock stairs led to the raised dais, a runner a shade darker than the blood red floors covering the middle of it and going all the way across the room to intricately-carved double doors. Statues about ten feet tall of a creature covered with a cloak holding a pointed spear stood on either side, the face covered with a wide hood. At least I assumed it was statues, but the slight shifting of the fabric said otherwise.

I chose to ignore that face for the sake of my sanity.

Everything else was just like the previous room, shiny

black stone walls rising high enough to prevent anyone from seeing the ceiling, and blood red stones with winking specks covering the floor. The air was different here, tension and expectancy that would've made me fidget if I had a body and that body was not broken thanks to the girl. I didn't have to wait long to understand why the room was charged with so much tension. The double doors crashed open, slamming on the walls an inch from the hooded statues.

A male, tall, regal, and dressed in dark red robes with a golden sash tied around his narrow waist rushed a female and a young girl inside the room. His golden hair with platinum streaks, very similar to mine in color, streamed behind him as he darted from side to side before pulling the doors closed and tugging a metal beam across them. The female was dressed similar, but it was more like the other-side-of-a coin fashion. Her robes were gold and the sash dark red, her long hair darker than night falling in waves down to her hips. She clutched the little girl to her chest, bunching up the gold and red dress the young child was wearing as she pressed the small head to her chest like she didn't want the girl to see what was happening.

I had the strangest urge to scream at them to leave the room.

"Wait and watch," the creature who dragged me here whispered inside my head like she could read my thoughts, freaking the hell out of me. It was the same voice from my nightmares. "This is what you wanted, is it not?"

Trepidation left me mute, so I didn't answer.

"This should hold them back for a while." The deep voice of the male echoed as he waved his hands over the doors to make runes flare over them soothed my heart, but it also broke it into a million pieces at the same time. My entire world stopped when he looked over his shoulder and revealed his face for the first time. "It won't be enough to stop them," he told the female.

"I should've known it was too good to be true. I should've realized Danu wouldn't keep her word and leave us alone." The female's voice tinkled like chimes, surprisingly calm despite the horror tightening her pretty features.

"Mamaidh," the young girl whimpered, clawing at her mother's dress. That's when everything I was trying to deny hit home for me with indisputable clarity.

The little girl was me.

Greedily, I absorbed my parents, trying to etch into my mind every little detail I could see. Until that moment, I never knew how starved I was to at least know how they looked. The body I couldn't feel was on fire, waves of heat wafting from the spot me and the creature were occupying. My mother's face snapped in our direction, her eyes so much like mine darting around in search of something. I wanted to call out to tell her I was there, but no sound came out.

A serene smile tilted her red lips at the corners and her tense shoulders relaxed.

"Bi sàmhach leanabh." Telling me to be quiet, she locked eyes with my father, and he rushed to her, wrapping an arm around her shoulders. "Bidh a h-uile càil gu math a dh 'aithghearr."

I knew she lied saying all would be well soon or I wouldn't be standing there, so messed up in the head I couldn't think straight. The double doors rattled, sending a shower of the black rock surrounding them to pepper the blood-red floors. It was like a ram was slamming from the other side and trying to break them open. The young version of me screamed and buried her head in her mother's stomach.

"I am ready. Show yourself," my mother said calmly to the empty room.

"Is this wise, mo chridhe?" Hearing him call her his heart shriveled what was left of mine.

"I knew it would come." She smiled at him with so much love it almost killed me. "I just did not expect it to be so soon." The doors were blasted again, that time creating cracks like spiderwebs on the walls. "Go. I will join you shortly."

I watched my father, helpless to stop or help him, as he walked up to one of the hooded statues. Bowing low, his long hair swept the red floors as he murmured something under his breath, then he faced it with his arms spread wide. The hood of the statue shifted, the hand holding the silver spear moving slightly to the side.

"I come freely. A life for a life." His voice rang out strong and clear.

The spear glinted as it sliced through the air before piercing him through the center of his chest. He didn't even make a sound, not even a gasp, but I was raging and screaming in my head. The doors bowed inward rattling the room again just as his body was engulfed in flames that reached for the unseen ceiling. At the same time, my mother shoved my younger self away from her, and I burst into an inferno, too. Both fires burned bright and hard for a long moment before blinking out. There was nothing left of my father.

I tried to understand what I was seeing, where my younger self last stood.

Me as an adult—just like I'd known myself to be as far as I could remember—was curled at my mother's feet. A tear trickled down her face as she looked at me, but she didn't reach for me. The creature that brought me here popped out of nowhere, creeping closer to my mother in the same gingerly fashion she did when I first met her. Again as a young girl with those freakish eyes.

"You will protect my child," my mother said without looking at the creature.

'You know what you have to do," the creature answered, greed sparkling in her gaze.

"I do."

"That is not all." The young girl licked her lips and rubbed her bony hands together. "I will need a stone from your throne as well."

"Mine and my husband's lives are not enough?"

"She will need help when the time comes. I shall only help to make her allies."

I watched numbly, as my mother walked to the thrones and punched the smaller one, breaking the top part like it was made out of paper. A small rock rolled to her feet and she swiped it, shoving it at the creature's face. The bony hand snatched it immediately, tucking it in the folds of the night shirt she was still wearing. I wasn't sure if that was how she always looked, or if she was manipulating me to see her like that no matter what.

My mother grabbed her long golden robes, ripping the bottom part away. Her sun-kissed legs were left bare, the robe covering her enough to not flash her ass at the creature. Two vicious-looking swords materialized in her hands when she turned to face the rattling doors. In one smooth move, she lopped off her long hair up to her ears. The black curls pooled at her feet before bursting into flames as well, leaving a pile of coal when the fire died out. The creature rushed forward, collecting them all in a pouch that also disappeared in the folds of the night shirt.

"I'm not sure this is wise, Ernmas," the young girl told

my mother, using her name for the first time. "You are a goddess, yet you are still one of the Tuatha Dé Danann. You cannot best the one that gave you life."

"I am Érenn, this is true. I am also the wife of Delbáeth, the fire shaped. The rightful owner of the Courtless throne." A chilling smile spread over my mother's lips. "I will join him, but that does not mean I cannot have fun before I do."

"You always loved a good battle, dear." The creature chuckled creepily, which made my mother grin.

The young girl snatched my arm where I was still curled unmoving on the floor, dragging me away as if I weighed nothing. A gasp passed my lips when she reached the spot I was watching from, and I suddenly had a body and was standing next to her in the same room. My muscles locked when I tried to rush and embrace her, but I couldn't move. My mother looked around, but I knew she couldn't see me either.

"You are the last one left, my girl. The heir to the throne. Make me proud. Tha goal agam ort, Myst." And although she was looking just left of my face, I knew she could sense me there.

"I love you too, màthair," I told her in a choked whisper.

I almost swallowed my tongue when a child came to existence right next to her, making me think I imagined the whole thing. It was me again, so I turned to glare at the creature standing next to me.

"I have a sister?"

"You do not."

"What the fuck is that then?" I stabbed the air angrily, and that only made the bitch laugh.

"You will not see, but you will hear." As soon as she said those words, I was blinded.

Secret Origins

Darkness met me, but I knew I was still standing in the same place, in the same room. Shouts and weapons being drawn were singing through the air while my heart was hammering so fast and hard, I had to press both hands at the center of my chest to stop it from breaking my ribcage. The creature's voice whispered from behind me, *"You have to run where no one knows who you are. You must forget until it's time."* It was followed by a splitting headache that caused the eyes to roll to the back of my head. The pain from my broken body returned tenfold, doubling me over.

"Hand over the child!" a female's voice snapped with so much power I screamed.

"Come and take her mother," my own mother spat in anger.

Laughter mingled with the maddening noise of a battle. Then nothing. The screams, the shouts, the clinking of metal. The silence was choking me, shriveling my lungs while my mouth was open in a silent scream. The voice whispered again, only this time from inside my head, *"You must forget until it's time."*

A weight settled at my temples and I bolted upright gasping for air.

Chapter Seventeen

"Myst."

My arms were sore where Fenrir had an iron grip on them while shaking me for all he was worth. I was still gasping and choking on my own saliva too much to be able to answer him or tell him to butt out, so I hung limply and allowed him to play with me like I was a rag doll. My head had developed its own heartbeat, and even my hair hurt. At least my body was only sore and not broken.

Small victories.

"Myst!" Fenrir growled loudly in my face.

"If you don't stop screaming, I will kick you in the balls, Fenrir." I groaned.

"Thank the Fates you are awake." Yanking me to his chest, he tightened his arms until I was suffocating again.

"I'm not sure being awake is a good thing right now." My voice muffled in his chest, I wiggled to tell him to release me. He didn't. "I can't breathe."

My ass bounced on the armchair when he dropped me like I was hot, but he didn't move away. The fear on his face was replaced with shock while I squinted at him, the light in the room burning my retinas after all the darkness. Fenrir took a step back, his jaw dropping to his chest. He opened and closed his mouth enough times that it was agitating.

"Are we playing pantomime?" With great effort, I even snapped my fingers at him. "Let me guess, a fish. No, wait! An asshole. That's it. What the hell is the matter with you?"

My answer was an accusing finger stabbed at the top of my head by the gaping Fae royal. Marius was also in on the game and playing a fish, only his face was devoid of all color and he was holding himself in a standing position by a tight grip on the back of the sofa.

"The two of you should become a couple. You are perfect for each other." While I eyed them warily, my hand reached up to gingerly prod at my head. "Oh ..."

The moment my fingertips brushed over cool-to-the-touch metal, I didn't have to look in the mirror to figure out the new shit I'd gotten myself into by not leaving things alone. Not to say I regretted knowing who and what I was, but really? Things couldn't get much worse, could they? Bolting upright, I rushed out of the living room, teetering peculiarly on my high heels as I searched the house for a bathroom.

Brushing past the General, who jerked back as if I was a demon, I could feel Fenrir right behind, Marius following, albeit from further away. Pushing doors open, I finally found what I was looking for, and flicking the light on, I planted myself in front of the mirror. The ceramic sink cracked when I tightened my hold on it, crumbling into dust between my fingers. My dusty hand reached up again to touch the silver circlet on my head with three deep red stones at the center.

"For fuck's sake." I groaned miserably, tugging hard without moving it an inch.

"He was telling the truth," Fenrir accused as if I knew everything and was hiding it from him on purpose.

The three of them were crowding the door, each of them wearing a different expression on their faces. Fenrir looked pissed like I'd killed his puppy. Marius looked like he was about to either shit his pants or faint but couldn't decide what he wanted to do. The General looked calculating and, dare I say, reassured. Why that was, it was anyone's guess.

"Who? The cow?" Ignoring all of them, I took another look at myself.

All I was able to see was my father's hair falling around my shoulders and my mother's eyes looking back at me. My peepers were a bit too large bulging out of their sockets, but I'd be damned if I ever let the three that were staring at me know how freaked out I was.

"So"—Clearing my throat, my feet shuffled uncomfortably for a second before I turned to face them again—"it would appear that my parents were royal." Fenrir's face darkened like a cloud of doom. "Who would've thought, right? Right?" My nervous snickering trailed off.

"That is the crown of the Courtless Throne," the Fae continued, his accusatory tone rubbing me wrong.

"You don't fucking say, Fenrir. Oh my goodness, how did this thing get on top of my head?" Glowering at him, I tugged on the circlet with everything in me, but apart from one strand of my hair, nothing else came off my head.

"This is not good news I assume?" The General frowned at Fenrir, but the Fae ignored him. Marius, on the other hand, was nodding adamantly, his neck cracking.

"Who are your parents, Myst?" All in all, at least Fenrir

was predictable. Like a dog with a bone, he would never just let shit slide.

"Were, Fenrir." The same pain from when I saw my parents look at each other with so much love returned, choking me even now. "Were, not *are*. They are dead now."

"Who?" A muscle twitched under his eye again, which made me wonder if a Fae could die from a heart attack. "Myst." Fenrir snapped me out of that daydream.

"The King and Queen of the Courtless Throne. There, happy now?"

"Names, Myst. Say their names."

"Érenn. Or Ernmas was my mother, and Delbáeth my father." It took a lot of swallowing to push the lump in my throat down.

The string of curses Fenrir started spitting out in English, as well as the language of the Old ones we used as Fae, made my ears burn and the other two flinch away from him. And I thought I had a potty mouth. He put me to shame. He might not have a stick stuck up his ass after all. Or I broke him. Anything was possible at this point.

"If there is something I should know, by all means share it, Fenrir. Don't be shy on my account." Leaning a hip on the broken sink, I crossed my arms over my chest. "And can you"—Twirling a hand to indicate my head, I huffed in frustration"—puff this thing out of existence? Or hide it so I don't have to look at it."

His wrists twisted while he mutely stared at me with an intense gaze, and I took an involuntary deep breath when his power washed over me. One quick look in the mirror told me he made the circlet disappear, although, I could still feel its weight on my head. That would take some getting used to. I should've thanked him, but I didn't.

"This changes many things," the Fae murmured, his eyes trailing up and down my body.

"In what way, apart from knowing what happened to me and who I am?" Brushing off his comment, I offered him a shrug. "I'm still Myst and have no intention of changing anything about myself or my life."

"The crown on your head, hidden or not, says otherwise, your highness." Mockingly bowing at me, his lips tilted in a chilling smirk.

"Keep that up, Fenrir. I might neuter you after all. You have the face to pull it off, too."

"You think I'm pretty?" Cocking an arrogant eyebrow, he grinned.

"For a girl?" Pretending I was considering it, I pursed my lips and gave him a once over. "Sure, if I was swinging that way."

"The two of you either fight it out or fuck it out," the General barked from behind Fenrir. "It seems to me we have an even bigger problem than those creatures I saw tonight. I will be damned if I let human lives be lost for freak-show politics."

"You did hear Fenrir say you have some of that freak show in your blood, didn't you?"

"I'm a human and I'll die as one. But if whatever he says is true, and I can use it to protect innocents, I'll take it." The old man squared his shoulders, which made him look taller than he was. He still had fire in him. Something that I now knew called to me for other reasons than just appreciating a warrior's spirit.

"We might need more than wishful thinking if we are to stop what's coming." After gnawing on my lower lip for a good minute, I sucked it up and said what I never thought would come out of my mouth. "I might have to go to Faerie to stop the annihilation of the human realm. They want my head, with or without the crown, and will stop at nothing to get it."

"There might be another way." Leave it to a Fae to give you a false hope.

Chapter Eighteen

Closing my eyes with a heavy sigh, I allowed my body to sink in the soft cushion of the armchair in the living room. Marius was sitting on the edge of the sofa as if his bony ass was on needles. His request for Fenrir to wipe his memories was shut down by the ass. I couldn't understand Fenrir's reasoning, but that was why we were there: to hear what the Fae thought was a good plan. The General leaned a shoulder on the wall refusing to sit down, and Fenrir paced.

It was making me dizzy.

I, on the other hand, had different plans and no intention of sharing them with the class. Male egos were for fools. My own ego might take a hit, but I'd rather continue breathing than have songs written about my prowess. Being outgunned was always a possibility in any battle. Being outsmarted was not, at least not if you played your cards right.

I had no intention of being easy prey.

"I should start from the beginning so we are all on the same page," Fenrir decided as I watched him through heavy lids turn to face all of us like a teacher in front of a class. I snorted, making him flick a dirty look my way. Mimicking zipping my mouth with an invisible zipper, I even locked it and threw away the key. He didn't appreciate the gesture, the ungrateful ass.

"Danu is the mother of us all." I had to grind my teeth when I heard the name so I didn't interrupt him again. "All Fae are known as Tuatha Dé Danann, or the children of Danu for that reason. She separated us into two courts to keep order. The children of Light or Seelie court, and the children of Darkness or Unseelie court. For long years, our people flourished and lived in abundance, until greed for power started corroding the courts." When none of us said anything, he folded his hands at the small of his back and continued to pace the length of the room.

It should've looked ridiculous.

But it looked hot and only made me squirm.

"Fighting and assassinations became an everyday thing in Faerie, sons killing fathers and daughters murdering mothers to steal their gifts. You see, the Fae learned that if you take the life of one of our brethren, you can siphon their powers into your own. The ultimate power became a coveted state of being and wars were fought at an alarming rate. That's when one of Danu's first daughters stood up to her mother and left the court of Light." His gaze flicked to me, but I didn't care how eager I looked. I was sitting ramrod straight at that point, soaking up each word coming from his mouth.

"Érenn walked away from her throne in the house of Seelie, many following right behind her refusing to kill or hate their kind for belonging to the Unseelie court. Soon after that, word spread that she made her own throne, the Courtless throne where all who didn't want to take a side were welcomed. A neutral zone, accepting everything and everyone who wanted to live a peaceful life instead of fighting or dying for power.

"Danu was not happy to be disobeyed by one of her dearest daughters, but she left her child to do as she pleased, expecting for Érenn to eventually come to her senses. Years passed and the Courtless throne was staying out of the wars more and more. One day, Danu faced her daughter determined to drag her back to her rightful place. In their battle, Danu nearly killed her daughter, but out of nowhere, Delbáeth blocked her killing blow and protected Érenn with his body. A royal from the Unseelie court, a fire shaped, covered the Seelie royal to save her life instead of taking it. Furious, Danu left swearing to end both their lives and hit them where it would hurt the most. Afraid for Érenn's life, Delbáeth hid them and no one has seen the Courtless Fae since. But, they kept balance and order, striking at anyone who disturbed the power in Faerie when no one expected it. All those joining the Courtless Throne followed them and it has been a legend ever since." Those piercing eyes pinned me on the armchair. "Until today."

"The bitch thinks I have a sister." For some reason that came out of my mouth.

"Do you?"

"No." With pursed lips, I leaned back in the chair to get rid of the kink in my back. "She thinks I do ... I guess."

After a deep breath, I told them everything that I saw when Marius was digging through my head. Fenrir looked a little green in the face when I mentioned the young girl who wasn't a girl at all, but I pushed through because I wanted it to be over and done with it. I hated the wistful tone of my voice when I spoke of my parents, talking faster than normal just to finish it quicker. The softening of the General's features didn't help either, so I glared at him while talking to snap him out of it.

"She just popped into existence next to my mother. I'm not even sure it was a child, it just looked like one."

"It could've been a number of Fae that joined the Courtless Throne coming to help her by taking your place." Fenrir rubbed his chin, completely lost in thought.

"If this bitch is the mother of all, wouldn't she know the difference?"

"From what I've heard of your father, he was a very smart male and determined to protect your mother at all costs. That's what the stories say, anyway." He shrugged, not realizing I was fighting tears. Damn, stupid emotions. "He would've been prepared for a situation like that."

"My mother told him it was time. Not the other way around."

"They worked together as a unit," the General rasped before clearing his throat. "That's what I took from everything you said tonight. You might've lost them before you had time with them, but they knew it and were prepared for it. You are still here thanks to their sacrifices."

"Rub a salt in the wound why don't ya." I really hated the human at that moment. "Do you have a wife, General?" I knew the answer but asked just to be a jerk.

"Not anymore." All emotions disappeared, leaving his face blank and stern. Thank fuck.

"Okay, so she killed my mother and took whatever it was that was pretending to be me." The headache was returning, so I pressed my fingers to my temples and massaged them. "Why come after me here if she had what she wanted? After that day, I haven't stepped foot anywhere near Faerie." Both hands dropped in my lap as I blew out a weary sigh. "I didn't want the stupid crown or the stupid Throne that got my parents killed. I still don't, but ..."

"But?" Fenrir leaned forward eagerly, and I had to frown at him to get him to back off.

"I have every intention to kill the bitch and her cow." My neck cracked loudly when I rolled it on my shoulders. "You can kill her, right?"

"Anything can die." It was the General who answered. "You just have to find a way to do it."

"He does have a good point," the Fae murmured, while Marius was trying to become one with the sofa. Poor shmuck.

"Leave it to a human to enlighten us." Fenrir chuckled, and I grinned at the old man to soften the sting of my words. "Well, General. I think we are about to test your bullets and see if they work on an actual goddess. Welcome to the freak show."

Chapter Nineteen

"Myst?"

"Bow." I was pointing at the tips of my boots while Fenrir was shooting daggers at me through his eyes.

"Myst ..." My name was growled as a warning, but I didn't budge.

"My mother was a goddess herself and I am the sole heir to a throne. Bow before you address me, peasant." I'd been needling him like that all day from the time I woke up.

"You do know I am a royal as well." Looking down his nose at me, he jutted his chin stubbornly.

"I don't know where you're going with this," I deadpanned, blinking at him in confusion.

"A royal does not bow to a royal ..." He blew a harsh breath through flaring nostrils, pinching the bridge of his nose with a thumb and a forefinger. "You don't even want the crown, or the throne."

"Yet, I still have the crown." Petting the invisible circlet that no one could see but I could feel sitting on my head, I grinned at him. "No one has seen my throne or the Courtless for centuries, so there are no rules binding me down. I can make up my own, and since I'm the one that keeps the balance, you will obey. Or until I can take this shit off my head. I'm not picky really. One or the other."

"Will the two of you stop?" the General growled from our right, his face reddening in anger unlike anything I'd ever seen from him.

"You are taking his side now?" I gaped at the old man. "You didn't even know him until yesterday."

"I'm not taking sides." He sounded as tired as Fenrir. "Come look at this and tell me what you think."

Walking past Fenrir, I peered around the General at a bunch of bullets that looked … well, just like bullets.

"What am I looking at?" Prodding at one with my nail, I made it almost roll off of the table.

"Look." The General snatched it before it dropped, bringing it to my face. "Can you see them?" He rolled the bullet between his fingers slowly. "On the casing."

"Ah, I see," Fenrir murmured over my shoulder, crowding me and sounding impressed.

I elbowed him in the gut.

"Back off, peasant." Taking hold of the General's wrist, I kept squinting at the bullet until what was on it gained clarity. Having my body broken into a heap of meat and shredded bone took its toll and I believed I was still healing. "Damn, General. I'm seriously impressed. No wonder you were ready to bite my head off when it comes to Marius."

Barely visible runes were interconnecting all around the bullet casing, making it look almost decorative and pretty if you had no idea what you were looking at. What I was seeing was a mean magic waiting to be unleashed on whoever the poor sucker was who ended up with a bullet hole in his or her body. The human was becoming indispensable by the minute.

"Well done, Marius." I turned to the mage, who was plastering himself to the wall in the corner and trying to stay as far away from me as possible. "You should be proud of yourself. This is genius."

Marius blushed, which made Fenrir growl.

"Seriously, Fenrir? The male wouldn't show me his dangly bits if I was the last female in all the realms and he was about to die of a case of blue balls. Stop scaring the help, peasant."

The General released a pained sound.

"Make yourself useful, go bring me something to eat before I faint. All this healing left me starving."

This time the old man looked ready to slap me, and after glaring for a good minute at my neutrally arranged features, Fenrir stomped off to bring me food while muttering to himself under his breath about stubborn Fae females being the death of him. I snickered at his back until he was gone.

"Okay, now that it's just us, tell me how the runes work." The words were hushed, though they came out in a rush. "There is no mage to trigger them with magic, not unless you have been breeding mages that will use the bullets without me being aware of it."

The General frowned, his intelligent eyes darting from my face to the place Fenrir disappeared turning a corner.

"He won't betray us on purpose, but he is a Daywalker oath bound to that cursed place. I don't want him knowing everything until I'm sure he won't feel honor bound to spill it at the Academy."

"I thought you two were ..." the human cleared his throat uncomfortably, dark pink shading his cheekbones. "It looked like ... I assumed ..." he stuttered, making him almost endearing.

"We fuck, General. It's what humans do too, yes?" His face went redder, and that had me giggling. "Just because he is hot and I want to jump his bones does not mean I trust him with everything."

Marius was choking behind us, hacking like a cat trying to cough out a hairball. Rubbing the back of my neck, I shifted on my feet. Fenrir would be back soon because he was not stupid. He knew I was up to something and I really didn't want to test our fragile truce just yet.

"Well?" Prompting the General, I kept glancing over my shoulder. "How do you activate the runes."

"It's fire magic," Marius answered. "When the bullet is fired, the spark sets them off to activate the magic. I placed a delay rune so it doesn't blow in your face when you fire it, but as soon as that burns out it'll eat through anything ... organic."

In other words, a skull or a body.

"This was your idea?" I was seriously shocked at how smart he apparently was.

"No, it was the General's. I only said I'd try, and well ... it worked."

"I thought you were a psychic mage. I guess I don't know enough about them." When the old man stiffened, alarms were triggered in my brain. "What are you two hiding?"

"I can do fire magic, too. Unlike other psychic mages." Meek, pale Marius lifted his chin as if expecting an executioner.

"Oookkayyy." Dragging it out, I was getting confused

about where this was going. "I feel like I'm missing something."

"Marius doesn't know of another one like him. That's why he was trying to hide among humans when you found him." The General searched my face when I finally understood they were worried I might flip because of that information.

"Pftt." Waving their worries away, I took the bullet from the General's hand and eyed it in fascination. "I couldn't care less if you sprout a tail Marius, just as long as you don't step on my toes or say a word outside this circle. But keep the information about you between the three of us." Both of them nodded grimly. "What's that saying the humans love so much? Ah, yes. You scratch my back, I'll scratch yours."

"I will rip his arm off and beat him with it if he tries to lay a finger on you." Fenrir stormed back with a paper bag dangling from his fingers.

"Look, the caveman peasant is here. He must've clobbered food on his way back." Before he changed his mind, I yanked the brown bag out of his hand and tore it open.

The scent of chocolate washed over my face as the paper ripped open revealing a box full of goodness-covered eclairs and another with a neatly, diagonally cut sandwich stuffed full of meats and salads.

"I think I'll keep you, peasant," I whispered reverently at Fenrir.

The open bag had me debating for all of two and a half seconds before I attacked the eclairs like a starving beast. I shoved a whole pastry in my mouth, puffing up my cheeks like a chipmunk. The eyes rolled to the back of my head when the chocolate, flaky dough, and creamy custard melted on my tongue. Embarrassing moans that came from me filled the silence, while the three of them watched me with horror and fascination. I didn't care at all.

"I think you just discovered the way to a woman's heart, son.' The General slapped a stunned Fenrir on the shoulder before walking away chuckling to himself.

Chapter Twenty

"Are you sure about this?"

Fenrir looked doubtful as he eyed the door of the pub I frequented to get peace of mind, a grimace on his pretty face. When the General said we would need to test the bullets before attempting to use them on the minotaur or on Danu, the first thing that came to mind was this place. Fates knew I'd killed enough assholes in the alley behind it to rate it as the prime spot for targets.

"It's not a palace or befitting my station, but I suppose it'll do." I sniffed arrogantly, almost ripping the heel of my boot off when it got stuck in a crack in the pavement.

Cleverly, Fenrir grabbed my upper arm to steady me while biting off his laughter, although I noticed his shoulders shaking when I squinted at him. I needed to check what was happening with my sight since I had to look through narrowed eyes to bring things into focus. It would have to wait until I killed the bitch and her cow first, though.

He followed as I pushed through the doors and braced

for the stench of sweat and stale beer to turn my full stomach inside out. The Fae hacked behind me when I beelined for the bar as fast as my feet would carry me. The bartended looked like he wanted to jump out of his skin, frozen like a deer in headlights as he openly stared at Fenrir. I looked too, but I couldn't see anything wrong with his appearance. He had his illusion cast, giving him platinum blond hair and sun-kissed skin. I was sure he looked less pretty to a human so he didn't attract too much attention, meaning we shouldn't have anyone gawking at all.

That was not the case.

"I should've known," Fenrir snarled, hunching his shoulders in such a way that I had to slap a hand on his chest to stop him from attacking.

"What the hell is the matter with you." Hissing at him, I was trying to see if the few humans sprinkled around the pub noticed his attitude. "Stop it, or you'll wait outside."

"A troll," he literally spat on the ground. I'd never seen him do that in my life.

"A what now?" Inching away so I didn't end up with spit on my boots, I looked around again searching for a troll. I found none.

"The bartender is a troll," Fenrir said slowly, almost like I was stupid and needed him to spell out things for me.

"He is most definitely not." Having had enough of his shit, I shoved him away and slid onto a barstool. "I've known him for a long time. He is human. He might stink like a troll, but he is one-hundred percent human." Waving my hand, I snapped said bartender from his frozen state by asking without words for my usual drink.

"You do know him?" Fenrir slid next to me, still glaring at the human. "What is his name?"

"Really, Fenrir?"

"From my observations"—I was already groaning about the incoming lecture but that didn't stop him—"I get the feeling you don't want to know names, besides from the supernaturals you might have to kill if they turn on you."

"Oh, wow. They'll build you a monument next to that crazy human. Einstein. That was really profound."

"They should." He was smirking. "And I'm right."

"Whatever. How unfortunate that I know yours." The bartender was taking his sweet ass time annoying the shit out of me.

"Do you know the General's name?" He was a pro at ignoring my jabs.

"No. General suits him just fine without additional words."

"A berserker. But you are right. It does suit him."

I had a feeling I was going to break a tooth because of how clenched my jaw was.

"You just learned the name of the mage, too." Fenrir hummed to himself, happy as a pig in mud.

"I don't know the name of the woman we sent with Leo to Sienna." There was a human to shut him up.

"A mother of half bloods. It counts."

"Is there a point in this, oh wise one?"

"He"—Jabbing a finger and startling the bartender, Fenrir huffed indignantly—"is a troll. And from now on, I'll be paying closer attention to anyone you refuse to know by name."

"You promised I would have no trouble, Myst." The bartender placed a glass of rum and coke in front of me with a shaking hand. Alcohol sloshed over the rim of the glass, soaking the napkin and his sausage fingers.

"Are you a troll?" My question caught him off guard

enough for him to blurt out a faint yes. "You gotta be shitting me."

Fenrir gloated next to me. I wanted to push him off the barstool.

"There is something different about you." For the first time, the human-turned-troll didn't run to the other side of the bar.

"Nah, it's just pretty boy here is killing my badass vibe, that's all. I'll still slice your head off if you piss me off."

"There is, there is." Undeterred, he moved even closer, looking me up and down with a puzzled expression.

"What the hell is the matter with him?" I mumbled under my nose, glaring at the bartender.

"He is a troll," Fenrir repeated pointedly.

"I heard you the first five times, Fenrir."

"Majority of them followed Érenn when she left the Seelie court," he whispered under his breath for my ears only.

"Oh … Oh!" My spine snapped straight, eyes darting around as if the cow would pop out of nowhere. Which was the case the two times I came across him.

"This is not good if he can sense you, Myst. It means your powers are leaking." He was stiff next to me as well. "I don't know why I didn't notice before."

"No female wants to hear she is leaking Fenrir, powers or no powers."

"We need to get out of here." He was already on his feet, my upper arm clutched in his hand.

"Take the back door, Myst. I haven't shifted in decades, but if you need help, I'll do it." The bartender shocked the shit out of me, rushing from behind the bar without looking to see if we followed.

Fenrir was already dragging me after the troll.

"Stop manhandling me." Snapping at the male, I snatched my arm back, now fully alert. "Go on, lead the way."

No one paid us attention as we bolted through a narrow hallway to the back entrance of the bar. The troll gripped the door handle and waited for us to reach him before he stuck his head out to look around. His body disappeared, snatched like he didn't weigh a good three-hundred pounds in human form, leaving the now-open door swaying on the hinges. The fast-approaching night was waiting for us through that threshold, the grating laughter coming from it not helping at all.

"Come out or I'll peel the skin off his bones." It was the damn cow.

"Go ahead, I do need new boots." Fenrir snapped his head my way and I shrugged. This is why I didn't want to know names. No one could use them against me that way.

Then the damn troll had to screw it up for me. "Don't do it, Myst. I'm not afraid to die, do mhòrachd."

Fenrir was still watching me, probably expecting a reaction when the troll called me "your majesty." My shoulder jerked in a shrug. "I told you, you should bow."

"The heir to the throne is in Faerie," The cow snarled. "This is a muddied bloodline that needs to be removed."

Okay, now he was getting insulting and he needed a lesson in manners. Plus, we'd come to the pub to test the bullets, after all. Snatching one of the guns tucked at Fenrir's lower back, I waved the barrel telling him to go first. I wanted to kill the cow, but I was not stupid. Fenrir could take more of a beating than me. With a shake of his head and a smirk, he pulled the other gun out and stepped in the alley. I followed right on his heels.

"History repeats itself." The cow, now doubled in size

from the last time I killed him, was staring daggers at us, the troll dangling from his hand. "Like mother, like daughter."

"You know what cow?" Fenrir sounded like he was in pain with his groan, and the cow snarled with hatred burning in his eyes.

"I was going to kill you. Now, I'm still going to kill you, but I will do it so slowly you'll be terrified to come to life again." The minotaur roared, shaking the ground at my feet.

I grinned at him with no humor.

"Let's dance bitch."

Chapter Twenty-One

"You really should stop calling him a cow." Fenrir panted, dodging hooves and punches as they swung at his head, which were coming from dinner-plate-sized fists.

"Why?" Dancing around him, I avoided the kick aiming for my own head. "He looks like one."

"He is a bull, so there is a difference." Ducking low, Fenrir managed to tuck his shoulder under the minotaur's arm and tackle him.

It was progress.

"Don't be a sexist. Typical male, just because your horns are bigger, that doesn't make you special, you know?" Taking a step back, I watched the huffing minotaur puff out clouds of air through his nostrils. The temperature dropped a few degrees when the bull attacked, and my own breath misted in front of my face.

"Cows give milk, which means they are human animals." Fenrir rubbed his shoulder, his feet inching ever closer to the troll cowering at the side of the wall. "And I do not have horns."

"Exactly. Which makes this cow right here useless." All our efforts to move the Minotaur a safe distance away to test the bullets had failed so far. Like he was attached by Velcro to us, he kept coming, which was really starting to piss me off.

He charged, catching me in the side with a hard kick.

"Motherfucker." Hissing in pain, I backed off and glared at the cow. "That will hurt for days."

In a blur, Fenrir slammed into the minotaur, both their bodies crashing into the brick wall and breaking through it. Luckily, the building next to the pub, across from the alley, had a shared laundry room, which was where they landed in a tangle of limbs. At least I was able to get the troll out of sight.

"Move." Yanking the bartender on his feet, I shoved him towards the still open back door of the pub. "Get inside and stay there."

"I can help." The idiot was struggling, digging his heels in when I tried to get him moving.

"Like you have helped so far?" Taking a firmer hold of his sweaty, hairy upper arm, I kept tugging him. "Get your ass inside and stay there."

"I didn't know," the troll pleaded when I literally frog-walked him to get him away from the alley. "Myst, I honestly didn't know or I would've told you."

"What are you talking about?" Growls and snarls were coming through the huge hole in the wall and making the entire ground move under my feet like I was standing on water.

"Who you were. If I had known, I would've told you I'm a troll." Using my distraction, he took hold of my hand and yanked on it. "You gotta believe me."

"That makes two of us." At his puzzled look, I snorted.

"It's a ... new development. Never mind, let's get moving. Unless you want the cow to really skin you alive. I can't babysit you, not when I have a cow to kill."

"I can shift." He shuddered. "It's been a while, but I'll do it to help you, and I'll rip his head off. I'm quite strong." Chest puffing out, he even sucked his beer belly in—or tried to anyway, but there was no hope for that sucker—and I honestly think he was expecting me to be impressed.

"Stay out of the way." With a weary sigh, I cracked my neck. "If you see us going down, then you can jump in. Not before."

That got him moving faster than I thought him capable of. Bolting through the back door and flipping around to turn and face me just inside of it, he gave me two thumbs up like an excited child. He was smiling from ear to ear too, which creeped me out.

Fenrir's body came out flying, his back hitting next to the pub's door before he dropped on his hands and knees. Black long hair brushed the ground before falling like a waterfall over his shoulders. Chest heaving, it took him a long moment to lift his face up, but when he did, I was worried his jaw would fuse together if he clenched it any harder. The runes kept pulsing and writhing deep red on his cheeks and neck.

The minotaur stepped through the hole, shaking his huge head as if to clear it.

Blood dripped from above his right eye, and his lower lip and torso was bathed with it, as well. Deep wounds cut off the streaks of swirling lines covering his upper body. His harsh breathing sounded like an engine sputtering to start. To my great pleasure, one of his horns had a large chunk on the end broken, hanging like an ornament and dangling next to his head.

It gave me an idea.

"No," Fenrir snarled.

"What?" I blinked innocently at him as I inched closer to the cow and pulled out my sword.

"I know that face, and no." Pushing up on his feet, the Fae tugged down his shirt as if he wasn't aware that he was covered in gunk and dust all over.

Prim and proper. That was Fenrir for you in a nutshell.

Scrubbing the back of my hand across my nose, and probably smudging my face further, I didn't suffer from those issues. I was pretty sure my hair was sticking out all over the place too. There were a few strands plastered on the side of my face that I couldn't be bothered to tuck behind my ear. Perfect material for royalty, I was sure.

"I don't know what you are talking about, Fenrir. There is nothing wrong with my face, and from what I can tell, it always looks the same." Stepping next to him, I searched for the best way to execute my plan.

"You are smiling." I chanced a quick glance at his face. "Not in a good way. It has trouble written all over it."

"Go stand with the troll then." I had to move while the cow still looked dazed or I would've missed my chance. "The two of you can cheer. I'm sure he can fish out some pompoms from somewhere. I don't even want to know what he has in the back of that pub."

"We should just shoot him." As usual, Fenrir ignored my brilliant ideas.

"We don't know how fast the delay rune will burn out. I need to be close enough to rip his heart out before he turns into a piñata." With pursed lips, I looked the minotaur up and down. "Too bad there will be no candy."

"You ate fifteen chocolate-covered eclairs not even an hour ago."

"Are you calling me a glutton?" The tip of my sword was under his chin, which made his body stiff. The cow looked confused, too, but he was finally watching us as if we were something to be wary off.

Fenrir's hands slowly lifted in surrender, palms up. "No, I just don't want you to be sick."

"Bullshit, but you owe me one more box of eclairs for the insult."

Fenrir is so easy to rile up. It worked in my favor, sidetracking the minotaur long enough that he wasn't expecting me to jump at him. Kicking back with one foot, I pushed myself off the wall, lifting the sword over my head. My body vaulted across the alley, and at the last second, I spun in the air slashing a crisscross on both sides of his head. A perfectly executed attack if I do say so myself. Two heavy thumps proceeded my boots down, hitting the ground, and that placed me face to face with the minotaur.

A cow now, since he had no horns.

"Much better." The grin on my face twisted his face in fury, and sparks flew out of his slanted eyes.

"Unbelievable." Fenrir groaned from behind me.

Tree trunk arms lifted as the cow tucked his elbows close to his body before punching out two-handed. His fist slammed into the center of my chest, breaking my ribs. It was lights out before I even hit the ground.

But it was worth it.

Chapter Twenty-Two

"You need to start being smarter."

Forcing one eye open, I tried to figure out what I was looking at. Ancient eyes peered down at me from a young face. Flicking a glance, I realized I was back in the empty room where I met the creature who showed me my lost memories. I also noticed I wasn't in pain, which was always a good thing. Lifting up on an elbow and a lot of blinking later, I brought the young girl into focus.

"Am I dead? Is that why I'm here?"

"Ridiculous." Huffing, she plopped on the blood-red floor next to me, curling her knees up and wrapping her bony arms around them. "It'll take more than a few broken bones to kill the daughter of Érenn and Delbáeth. Not to say that you can't permanently be put out of commission. In which case, they will find a way to remove the crown and then you can be killed."

As a reaction to her words, my hand was already up, my fingers brushing the circlet still sitting on top of my head. The weight of it was not as heavy here as in the human realm, so I had forgotten it was even there until she mentioned it. Back where the cow was probably grinding my bones at the moment, I felt its presence as if I was wearing a hat the whole time. A slight pressure that would give me a headache with prolonged use type of thing.

"Can I go back now?" It wasn't like I was looking forward to being in pain, but I didn't want Fenrir to end up hurt, or Fates forbid dead. Could he die at the hands of the cow? "I was kind of in the middle of something. You know, getting beaten up."

"I didn't call you here." The creature was eyeing me as if I'd sprouted a second head. "Nonetheless, it is good that you came. I forgot to tell you a few things about your origins. Why they were a secret."

"We can chat another time. When I'm not about to be turned into pulp. Scouts honor." I even lifted my hand like a good girl, which only made her glare at me.

"The Unseelie royal will keep you alive at the cost of his own life. You have time." She shook her head, her golden hair bouncing around her shoulders as a small smile played on her thin lips. "So much like your father, that one."

"If he gets hurt, I'll rip your throat out." I threatened through clenched teeth. "Repeating it for eternity if I have to."

"Let us not waste time then." I didn't like the look on her face. It was like she knew something I didn't, and it set my teeth on edge.

"Speak and get it over and done with," I prompted her by twirling a hand in her face. "I have places to be, people to kill."

"After your mother joined your father in the afterlife, Danu took the child and raised it as her own." Her voice got a faraway quality, which made me squirm. This looked like it might take a while. "You see, Danu wanted to get her favorite daughter back. She lost Érenn due to her own stubbornness and arrogance. With the child, she can redo things, change history."

"I was the only child." That much I knew for certain, and I knew it deep in my bones.

"Danu knew that, too. Until your powers started flaring up and brought her attention to you." She wiggled a finger at me. "I left you with the Daywalkers in Sienna for that purpose. Their wards, along with the Old one keeping it standing with his life, were enough to hide you from her notice."

"Soren? You let that nut case hide me? No one can keep him awake long enough to have a full conversation with the Dragon Blood. Well until Francesca. She got his ass into gear alright." I snickered at the picture in my mind.

"I could've sworn as long as you were in Sienna, Danu would never know about you. In that I have failed." She looked so remorseful that my mouth opened, and I was spilling my guts in no time.

"Umm, about that." More squirming was involved at this point. "I left Sienna decades ago."

"You what?" She was on her feet, her voice coming from all sides and nowhere all at once, and it was loud enough to burst my ear drums.

"Hey!" I jumped up, too, glaring at her. "Don't you scream at me. I had no idea who or what I was, and they were poking through my head. What the fuck did you expect me to do? I had enough nightmares to know all too well I didn't want to remember anything. So, fuck you and your fucking plans. How about that?"

The vast room rocked on its foundation, forcing both of us to stumble. My arms shot to the sides as I tried to balance on my heels, while the creature stood there with daggers shooting from her eyes. Not a hair moved on her head. It was as if she had somehow defied gravity. Stupid creatures, and stupid Faerie realm.

"Well, what is done is done," she said on a sigh after our staring match. "Now that Danu found out about you, she believes that there were two of you. The child she raised follows her orders to the T. She is the perfect daughter, the one she always wanted. You, on the other hand"--Her head tilted to the side in that bird-like manner, and the movement prickled my skin—"are a wild card. Someone she has no control over. And when you come across an obstacle that can mess up your plans and all your hard work, you remove it."

"Great. She'll have a hard time removing this speed-bump." I pushed the words through clenched teeth, still pissed off that she yelled at me. "I have no intention of being easy prey. Danu might eventually kill me, but she'll have a hell of a time until I kick the bucket. I can promise you that much." Rubbing a hand over my face, I groaned. "Talk about family drama."

"All is not lost." The creature was trying to placate me, which irritated me more. "I made a plan after we saw each other last."

"We only saw each other once," I pointed out.

"That's what you think."

"Let me hear your plan so I can go back and ignore it." Getting tired of it all, I kept my eyes closed. I knew I'd be looking over my shoulder after her comment to make sure she wasn't stalking me. Look at me, raising up in life.

First a crown, now a stalker.

"Donn Cúalinge, the minotaur, has not told Danu anything yet." She looked so proud at her words that I got suspicious straight away. "He does not want to displease her. Her punishments are harsh." With a shrug of her shoulder, she continued. "Danu sent him to find where the flair came from and to remove it from existence. The Bull of Danu himself reasoned that Érenn had two daughters, and that was all he told her, as well as that you would be easily removed because you are so weak. It is good for Danu to believe this. Before you face her, we have a lot of work to do. Until then, you must kill Donn Cúalinge. And you must make it look like someone else did it."

"What you are saying is that I'll have the scars and bruises from it, but someone else will have the glory, huh."

"You want glory, child?" Her freaky black eyes had a manic glint in them that scared the shit out of me. "Or do you want to take your rightful place and avenge your parents?"

"I'm not placing this hot ass on any throne." Slicing a hand through the air, I made sure we were on the same page. "Avenging my parents, on the other hand … you got yourself a deal. Plus, I hate the bitch Danu and her cow."

"We shall see. All in good time." Smiling, she was rubbing her hands like some cartoon villain. "Kill Donn Cúalinge. After that is done, we must face the shadows of torment."

"You're not selling it, girl. Your sales pitch sucks."

"We will destroy everything Danu has been plotting for millennia's, step by step." Not hearing a word, I had a feeling she was lost in her own crazy head. "Oh, how I look forward to seeing the look on her face when it is done."

"Okay, psycho. I'm not playing your games. You do what you have to do, and I'll just go be awesome or something … faraway from here."

"Yes." I jumped at her shout. "Go kill the Bull of Danu.

We will take it one step at a time. I will keep Danu occupied enough until there is no stopping what's coming for her."

"As long as you keep your crazy ass away from me, we're good."

"After Donn Cúalinge is no more, keep your head down. I will come to you when it's time and the next phase shall begin. And by no means"—The creature crowded me, bringing her face so close to mine our noses touched, and even though I was taller, I didn't dare wonder how she managed to do that—"let anything remove that crown from your head. Am I clear?"

"Got it. Kill a cow, keep the crown. Crystal clear." I wanted to be out of that place yesterday.

"I have waited a very long time for this." The glee was palpable, and it raised goosebumps on my arms. "Now, go."

The room started fading, but it left a very heavy, unsettled feeling in the pit of my stomach. Somehow, I got myself thrust into a shitstorm, and it wasn't even one of my own making. Gods were trying to kill each other or take each other's place by using me as a bone thrown between hungry dogs. All I wanted to do was stay alive. I could do that, right?

The odds did not look like they were in my favor.

Chapter Twenty-Three

"I should've stayed with that loony girl. Now that I think about it, I can totally deal with that type of crazy. Much better than this. Ouch." While talking to myself, my hands fleeted over my body to make sure I was still in one piece.

"Myst?"

Fenrir was so busy fighting the minotaur that he called out without turning to check on me. I was so sore, and I had every intention of allowing him to keep at it while I stayed stretched out on the disgusting ground. Not even the stench bothered me as long as I didn't have to move. That was until I turned my head to the side to see what I missed.

"Stop!"

My shriek jerked Fenrir's arm to the side, the fired bullet ending up pinging off something from behind the bull, ricocheting back, and forcing him to duck while cursing up a storm. The troll braved coming out when I was busy chatting with crazy girls, darting around the minotaur to distract him while Fenrir almost made the cow go boom. No, there would be no piñatas tonight. The General could test his bullets some other time.

"Don't you dare shoot him." I scrambled to my feet, wincing and grimacing from the pain. I felt like a semi had hit me, reversed, ran me over, then hit me again. "There will be no shooting tonight."

"I think she hit her head," the troll huffed, darting diagonally and barely avoiding the minotaur's swinging arm.

"I can still kill you, so don't think I won't." My threats fell on deaf ears.

"My name is Gregor." He grinned a second before a fist caught him to the side of his head and he pirouetted around, bouncing his head off the opposite wall. His body dropped like a rock, but it left him out of the fight.

"I don't get it," I deadpanned to Fenrir.

"He heard us talking about how you don't want to know the names of those you might have to kill." Fenrir grimaced as if he finally smelled something foul and he hadn't been present in the alley of deadly odors until now.

"That's because you have a big mouth." At his cocked eyebrow, I realized my slipup. "Not that you were right or anything. But he doesn't know that, does he?"

"Right." He did not look like he believed me. "Why aren't we shooting? I thought we were going to test the bullets. It's the perfect opportunity."

"We had a change of plans." Finally seeing my sword, I rushed forward and snatched it off the ground. I must've dropped it when I was knocked out. "The cow needs to die. As in dead, dead. Permanently removed from the board game instead of just put to the side for future use. You know? No flicking it off."

"I get it." Fenrir's voice was dryer than a desert.

"Not just dead until he comes to visit again," I added to make sure he really got it and wasn't just saying that he did.

"I know what dead is, Myst."

"Do you?" Rolling my shoulders, I hyped myself up to get into a serious fight with the cow. "Do you really? You almost shot him, which would've brought him back in twenty-four hours. It's his thing, and that's how long it takes him each time."

"You were out, I was continuing with the plan that you specifically told me not to botch up for you. In those exact words."

"Well we have a new directive now, get with the program." Puffing a few harsh breaths like a fighter before a match, I did a few slices with my sword in front of me. In all honesty, I wasn't looking forward to a one on one with the cow. He was using this time to catch his breath too, but he looked pissed.

"Who gave the new directive?" I had to push Fenrir away when he thought it was a good idea to step in front of me like a living shield. Males.

"Remember the creature I told you about. The one that looks like a young girl?" His head jerked so hard my way I swore I heard his neck crack. "Yeah, that one. She's the new sheriff in town, apparently. And don't look at me that way, Fenrir. That one is crazier than crazy, and I don't want to be on her bad side. If she says kill the cow permanently, I'll even milk it for her."

"You will do no such thing."

"What, you don't want to watch me …" I mimicked jerking off with my hand, which made it look like Fenrir was ready to explode. "Good, you are pissed. Now help me kill it."

Secret Origins

With a roar, Fenrir plowed into the minotaur, catching him off guard. The damn bull stumbled but kept standing. His huge arms wrapped around Fenrir's waist, lifting him off the grown before he tossed him aside. It had to chafe on the Fae's pride that he couldn't use his powers tonight, and especially since it was ordered by the General. Sounds drifted from the street beyond the alley, a car alarm going off and screeching when the impact of Fenrir hitting the ground shook everything around us.

He did look hot when he was jealous.

"Let's end this, cow."

I didn't wait for another second. Pushing off the ground with both feet, I spun and started kicking, slicing, and punching everywhere I could reach on the minotaur's body. The bull might be three times my size and twice as strong, but I was faster. Taking advantage of my petite frame, I danced circles around him, forcing him to clumsily flip around and search for me. Each opening I had I took, turning his bare torso into kebob meat. Chunks of his skin and muscle fell, hitting the ground with wet, squelching sounds.

He roared so loud I lost my balance.

My back hit the wall behind me, and all I could think was the General would be pissed because there was no way humans didn't hear this. The cow sounded like Godzilla was attacking the city, and although it was late, there were still enough people out and about. The only thing worse would be if someone used their phone to take a video of us before we caught sight of them.

A fist almost cracked my skull, banging the back of my head in the brick wall.

Stars twinkled behind my closed eyelids while I

continued slashing blindly with my sword to keep the minotaur from killing me. A shadow moved behind the bull's wide shoulders, but I was too dazed to see what it was. He also kept breathing harshly, his putrid breath wafting in my face strong enough to almost make me faint.

"End this." Fenrir's voice came from behind the minotaur just as the Fae wrapped both arms under the cow's armpits, locking his hands behind the hornless head.

He was keeping the cow stationary for me so I could rip out his heart. Ghost pains from my shattered fist tingled on my now-healed hand. The bull was struggling, his flailing strong enough to dislodge Fenrir at any moment. I had no time to hesitate, and remembering the manic glint in the creature's eyes when she spoke about what was coming told me if Danu knew exactly who I was, dying at the minotaur's hand would be a mercy. If I couldn't reach his heart with a hand, I would chew through his ribcage with my teeth.

I had no intention of dying. Not yet.

With a scream, I cocked my arm back, but something strange happened. All the runes that I hadn't seen since my sex marathon with Fenrir flared to life. The darkness in the alley lit up with red as if resembling the pits of hell. Fenrir's startled gaze was wide, and I really didn't want to know how I looked. Unfortunately, the cow had very large, very black eyes, which of course he turned on me. The world stopped as I faced myself in the glossy, terrified gaze that was acting as a mirror.

Blonde hair twirled around my head like a living thing, the long strands curling like snakes in the air. My eyes were glowing like two stars on pale skin that was covered with deep red pulsing runes. My cheekbones were pointed and sharp, adding to the otherworldly quality of my appearance. The circlet on the top of my head was bigger, the spikes sticking out from my hair glinting and reflecting the glow of my runes.

But nothing was as horrifying as my smile.

Blood red lips were tilted at the corners, promising things worse than death.

My heart stopped when I saw what I had become.

Just as my hand punched through the chest of the minotaur, the sound returned with a whoosh. His face was frozen in terror, and he didn't make a sound as I curled my fingers around his pulsing organ, ripping it out of his body with a squishy wet sound. The life left his dark eyes, leaving an empty shell hanging from Fenrir's arms, but the heart was still pumping in the palm of my hand. My fingers went limp and I dropped the organ at my feet.

"Fenrir?" The voice coming out of my mouth was one of a young, lost girl. "What is happening to me?"

"I got you." Dropping the body of the minotaur, he caught me in his arms when my knees gave out. "Myst, it's okay." He brushed the hair off my face, his worried gaze flicking over my features. "Just breathe, mo chridhe."

Wrapping my fingers around the wrist of his hand, I stopped his fidgeting. Hearing him call me his heart, just like my father did to my mother, tightened my chest and prevented me from breathing. It scared me more than seeing my reflection in the minotaur's eyes. Would we have the same fate as my parents? Would we have a chance at love, or would a deity force us to sacrifice ourselves to please the gods? How much time did I have to keep this males love until the Fates ripped us apart?

I swallowed the panic choking me.

"I'm fine, just a moment of insanity." Offering Fenrir a cocky smirk, I pushed him away and jumped to my feet. "The cow stinks like hell and it scrambled my brain."

"Myst ..."

"I'm serious, Fenrir. I'm good." And just to sell it better, I lifted my foot and stomped on the heart until I grinded it to pulp. "One asshole down. Let's go tell the General what happened before we have to start thinking of how to kill the next thing coming for my head."

"It's okay not to be strong all the time." The Fae was still poised to catch me if I went down. "I will be your strength when you need a moment. You can lean on me when you need to catch your breath. There is no shame in that."

"Got it." Flashing him a tight smile, I started moving. "But I'm good. Nothing can bring this awesomeness down, Fae. You should know that by now."

He didn't say a word, but the heat of his body at my back made my shoulders relax. There was no reason to voice my worries to him because, knowing Fenrir, he would go all cavemen on me. I needed room to breathe and if he started suffocating me, I knew myself well enough to know I would run. I didn't want to run from him. That fact was something that surprised me, and I wasn't sure if it was a good or bad thing. It might cost him his life.

"I'm not going anywhere, so don't even try," Fenrir grumbled from behind me as we reached my car.

He knew me better than I knew myself at times.

"I don't know what you're talking about."

Jumping in the car, I started the engine and zoomed out of the parking lot before Fenrir had his door closed. I didn't tell him about the creature mentioning shadows of torment. That shit show could wait another day. I'd deal with it when it came. Until then?

A cow was dead. Danu had no idea where I was, and

the damn crown was still attached to my head. I'd call that a victory.

Who knew poking at your secret origins could bring out so much shit, most of which should've probably been left buried?

Not me, that was for sure.

More by Maya Daniels

vinci-books.com/investigated

Monsters love it when prey stumbles into their lair—until their den becomes the cage.

Franky Drake, an undercover agent, must navigate the halls of Daywalker Academy. As secrets unravel and lines blur between loyalty and betrayal, she finds herself caught between duty and a dangerous desire, especially when the academy's most lethal vampire offers his aid. With a war on the horizon, can she prevent bloodshed, or will the price be too high to pay?

Turn the page for a free preview…

Investigated: Chapter One

"He is cutting through the back."

My partner Aiden growls next to me, his eyes trained on the back of the shifter we've been chasing halfway around town for the last hour. My arms are pumping, the breath coming out in short puffs of steam around my face. On the bright side, it's nice not to feel the chill of early winter. On the other, I can really use a break and get this sucker.

The call came in anonymously that the wolf shifter is seen exiting a witch's house, covered in blood. He is dressed all in black, so it's difficult to see the evidence of it, but I can smell the coppery scent that follows him like an arrow pointed at his head. In the last month, the number of calls has increased, the killings have doubled, and we can barely keep up with it. Adrenaline surges though me, the need to get ahold of him to get some answers pushing me faster than normal. We haven't been able to get one peep from anyone about what is feeding this violence between the species.

Not bothering to answer Aiden, I veer off to the right,

barely missing clipping his shoulder with mine. The last couple of weeks, my depth perception has been shit. I'm lucky if I get my ass in a chair without missing the whole thing and landing flat on my back. But that's a problem for another day. Right now, as I wheeze past homes, jump over fences, and trespass through people's back yards, I need to concentrate on getting this guy. Not because I have something to prove, or for some sort of righteous notion of doing something right. As sad as it may sound, it's because I've screwed up more times than I can count lately, and I'll get suspended if the guy gets away.

Aiden heads off to the left, I'm assuming to try and cut off the shifter from further ahead. The bark of a pissed off dog lodges my heart in my throat, but I'm gripping the wooden planks of the tall fence, already catapulting my body over it. Disappearing behind a two-story home, I see just a glimpse of the guy I'm after, and it propels me faster. Adrenaline rushes through me again, my fingers tingling with the weird energy that has been going to town on me and wreaking havoc on my body.

"Get the guy, Franky. Then think about your messed up life." Huffing under my breath, I zip by an open sliding door, hearing chatter and laughter coming from inside one of the homes.

It must be nice, I think gloomily to myself. *To live a life ignorant of all the ugly that hides in the shadows waiting to pounce on you at any given moment.* I don't begrudge them their innocence. I envy it. It's not their fault I was born as a hybrid creature of the night, something they believe is just a figment of their imagination. And fate, the cruel and wicked witch that she is, couldn't just land me in one of the species. No, my parents had to be the rebels of the supernatural world and mix genes. What was supposed to be a one night stand to scratch an itch ended up with a weirdo like me bumping uglies with the rest of them.

Mixed species are looked down upon in our world. The pure blooded love to say it's because we have a higher tendency to go feral, or turn psychopathic. The truth of it is, hybrids get to have mixed powers from both species, and when they reach their prime, they are more powerful than any pure-blooded creature. They can't control us, so they came up with a way to erase us from our world. Hence, there are not many of us around. I assume that they just kill the product of the coitus before anyone finds out, but I could be wrong. Hell, I am wrong more times than not, and that's why I am running after a shifter tonight. Like that time when I thought a guy was really nice only to find out he was a psycho luring me to his den so he and his buddies could have some fun. Needless to say, he misjudged the situation as well as I did. He died, and I ended up on the radar of Andrius Roberti, the meanest motherfucker of the supernatural world.

And, wait for it…my boss.

I was only sixteen at the time, but he kept me on a short leash, threatening to lock me up or kill me if he felt like it. For years, I was looking over my shoulder, and even under my bed, thanks to him. As soon as I turned twenty-one, he showed up and swept me away into his organization, not giving me the option to gracefully decline, which I had every intention of doing. I even practiced what I was going to say in front of a mirror. It sounded great and quite respectable to my ears, until Andrius showed up and pointed his finger at the open car door waiting at the curb.

The Supernatural Agency for Accord is his baby. He only takes those that have proven their worth in his eyes as part of his team. All of them are pure-blooded, their powers manifested, with years of training under their belts. Everyone is praying before they fall asleep that the Agency doesn't come knocking on their door. Not that it knocks. One agent will show up at your door and give you two options. Either go peacefully or die right there in your granny robe and fuzzy slippers. I'm not really the robe and slippers type, but I'm just saying. He collects the best of the best to keep the order the supernatural groups agreed on.

When the supernaturals decided to out themselves to the humans, all hell broke loose. My world collided with theirs and, from the stories I've heard, it was a blood bath. We are stronger, more powerful, and nearly impossible to kill, but the humans have one great advantage. Their number. They outnumber us a thousand to one and it worked in their favor. The Purge, as they call it, happened, and if we were to stay alive we had to agree to keep in the shadows and not mingle with humankind. Our town was created, protected by wards no one could breach, and the Agency was established to keep everyone here in line. No one leaves this town, apart from a select few. Andrius is as close to a god as anyone can ever get in our world, and his team is as feared and as powerful as him. All of them are legends. He collected the strongest, most powerful warriors.

And me.

Rounding a corner, the stitch on my side pulls me from the trip down memory lane just in time to be able to duck and roll, missing the flying fist to my face. My hip and shoulder take the brunt of the impact with the unforgiving ground as I tumble on the sidewalk, pebbles digging into my palms. Ending up in a crouch, my eyes widen when the sole of a size eleven boot obscures my vision. Jerking back, landing on my ass, I scramble like a crab to put distance between myself and the damn shifter that apparently got sick of running.

Just my luck.

A wicked grin splits his face, his eyes lighting up with the strength of his wolf. Usually, they would be the eyes of a predator prepping itself for a fight. Not this guy. There is a crazed glint in his gaze, something I haven't seen even on a rogue gone feral and lost to his animal side. It almost looks like desperation. It gives me a pause, enough time for his other foot to connect with the side of my head. A burst of colors blooms behind my eyelids from the power he put in that hit. My face scrapes on the pavement, but I'm already pushing up and turning to face him. I regret my decision not to carry my weapons tonight, something this jerk should be grateful for.

"If I knew it was a mongrel chasing me, I would've stopped running a long time ago." His voice is gravelly, more animal than man, and bile rises in the back of my throat when he adjusts his junk.

"Aww, look at you." Sweetness is dripping like honey from my lips. "Such a sweet talker. I bet the ladies love it, huh?"

"Roberti must be desperate if he is sending you after me."

"Or you just suck dude, so he figured that's all you're worth." Shrugging nonchalantly, I eye him for weaknesses. Oh, how I wish I had my daggers. "You think you are the top of the food chain because you killed a witch? Hate to break it to ya, but my guess is no. It just makes you a liability we can't afford."

"I killed no one!" Taking a menacing step towards me, he grinds his teeth. "She was dead when I got there."

"Rightttt!" My hands are tingling bad, and my entire

body is quaking with the need to knock his ass out. "And you were not escaping. You were just going for a night run after having a bath in her blood."

"Exactly." Baring his teeth, he swings at my head again.

I'm ready for it this time, so I block with my forearm, stepping in instead of pulling back so I can come face to face with him. They always underestimate the girl. My tall, thin frame makes them think I'm easily breakable, I guess. Why that happens is beyond me, but I'll take it. Shoving my hand flat on his chest, I send all the pent-up energy zapping through him. His body convulses, his manic eyes rolling to the back of his skull. A scream is ripped from me when claws tear at my skin. The shifter's face starts morphing into his wolf, and with just a second to spare, I push myself off him and stumble back.

Dropping on all fours, a dark gray wolf the size of a pony stares at me from two feet away. The same crazed look is swirling in his eyes, his top lip curling over sharp canines as long as my pinky. Saliva is dripping down his fur, and his sharp claws, one coated in my blood, scrape the pavement as if they twitch with the need for more.

The entire left side of my body feels like it's on fire. My blood is flowing freely, drenching my shirt and pants. The scent of it mixing with the witch's blood still saturating the air around him only makes the wolf wilder. I can see it in the posture of his body, the slight hunch of his back legs, and the pinning of his ears on his skull. He's preparing to pounce. With nothing left but to fight for my life, I place my weight on the balls of my feet, bending my knees slightly and bracing for it.

A horrified scream makes both our heads jerk in that direction. I have never in my life heard a sound filled with so much terror. The blood curdles in my veins. Without a second thought, I bolt in that direction, forgetting all about the beast that is preparing to rip me to shreds, and the reason why I am facing off with a crazy shifter in the middle of a street to begin with. To my shock, the wolf is running parallel with me, loping down the street with his gaze trained in the distance. All my pain and injuries are forgotten together with the fleeting thought that Aiden is nowhere to be found. It all gets lost in the rushing of the blood in my ears, my feet barely touching the ground from the urgency I feel burning in my chest.

Rounding a corner, I skid to a stop. Two shadows twist and twirl around a lump in the middle of the street. A hand reaches toward the sky from the crumpled person on the ground, as if warding off the waving shadows. The wolf next to me releases a sound between a growl and a whine, and its ears go back, flattening on its skull before turning around and disappearing into the night. I can't look away from the scene in front of me to even worry that my suspect is getting away, or what that means for me and my future in the Agency.

The darkness around the shadows is all-consuming, sucking in the light from the lampposts scattered down the street. The eerie silence creates a buzzing in my ears that only amplifies the rushing sound of the blood in my veins. Only my gasping breaks the stillness around me, and I realize too late that I shouldn't stand like an idiot in the middle of the road for anyone to see.

The movement of the shadows stop and although I can't see its eyes or face, if it even has any, I can tell when it turns its attention on me. The short hairs on the back of my neck stand on end, and my fight or flight instincts kick in. My gaze is locked on the lump on the ground, slowly disappearing from view as if being erased from this life like it never existed. The horror of that thought keeps me rooted on the spot, even when everything in me screams that I should run. The lump disappears, and the shadows condense into one before heading straight at me. Heart hammering in my chest, my entire being numbs from the crippling fear that overtakes all rational thought. Keeping my eyes open, I stare at my death, now only inches away from me.

All the air is pushed from my lungs when something barrels at my side, sending me rolling for a few feet. The rough pavement shreds all of my exposed skin while I'm skidding on it, unable to stop the momentum. My head cracks on the sidewalk, the sickening crunch too loud to my own ears. Through blurry eyes, I see the shape of a man looming over me, as if checking if I'm still alive, but I can't see his face or his clothing. I know for certain it's not my partner, the wide shoulders and powerful arms definitely not matching Aiden's swimmer physique. It's all fading rapidly as I taste acid in my mouth. The last thought that rolls through my mind is, *'Shit, the shifter got away'.* But then another thought quickly follows, making me chuckle in my mind. *Andrius can't blame me, because I'm going to be dead.* I lose my fight with consciousness with a smile on my face.

Investigated: Chapter Two

"She let it get away." Aiden points an accusing finger at me as I purse my lips.

Unfortunately for me, I didn't die. The jerk pointing a thick finger at my face found me on the street and brought me to Andrius before dumping a bucket of water on my head. So, here I am, drenched like a rat after a flood and dripping water all over the expensive rugs covering the floors of Roberti's office. By the reddening of his face, I'm quite positive he does not appreciate it. Neither do I, but I can't tell him that right now.

"What are you, five?" Glaring at Aiden, I poke at the rips on my shirt. "You found me unconscious, dumbass. I didn't let anyone get away. As I said..."

"Yes, we all heard what you said." Clenching his meaty fists, Aiden vibrates from his anger. "Shadows materialized out of nowhere and made something disappear." My unwilling partner does not hide his dislike of me. He never has, as long as I've known him.

"And you think what? I made that shit up because a

shifter got away?" My own anger spikes up at his accusation. He might've taken offence when he asked me out and I laughed in his face. It was one of those foot in the mouth moments for me because I thought he was joking. Apparently, he was not. Immortals hold grudges for a very long time, I'll say that much.

"Enough!" Andrius barks, cutting anymore arguments with just that one word.

Glancing at my boss's face, my heart skips a beat at the intent stare he has trained on me. Dropping my eyes to my feet like my boots are the most fascinating thing in the world, I swallow the panic that's trying to overwhelm me and push aside my need to stare him down in a challenge. Submissive I am not, but neither am I stupid. I fucked up. He is going to kick me to the curb now. It isn't like he hasn't promised that a few times already. This had been my chance to show him I'm at the top of my game and I screwed up more than ever.

My palms are sweaty as I keep ripping at the shredded shirt. Not a trace is left from my injuries. I heal fast, yes, but not this fast. Something happened on that street tonight. Something I can't explain, and even when I try, none of them believe me. Hell, I don't even believe myself, and I was there. And who the fuck was that guy that saved my life? I don't need anyone to give me a rundown of what happened. If he wasn't there, I would've been dead right now. Biting on the inside of my cheek, tasting my own blood, I keep my mouth shut. That's the least of my problems. After being in the agency for ten years, I have no idea what I'll do with my life when Andrius tells me to pack my bags. I don't fit in with the human world, even if I could walk out of the wards. Neither do I fit in with the supernatural one, and those same wards hold me hostage.

"Get out!" The softly spoken words pack so much power that my feet are moving before my brain even registers what I'm doing.

Aiden is out the door so fast I feel a breeze ruffle the short hairs that have escaped my braid around my face. I follow right on his heels, holding my breath. Andrius said get out, but not get out of my building. That's a good thing, right? Mind reeling with where I can make myself disappear until my boss calms down, I reach for the door so I can close it behind me, one foot already out the door.

"Not you, Drake. Get your ass inside and close the door."

I was so close, so damn close to escape I can taste it. Sucking in a deep breath, sending prayers to anyone that will listen, I blow it out slowly as I close the door in front of me and turn to face him. Not daring to lock gazes, I stare at his chin. My boss is a perfect example of an immortal being. His physical appearance, which is stuck in his mid-thirties when most of us reach our prime, can lure the unsuspecting fools into a sense of false security. The smart-pressed suit molds to his large frame like a second skin. Refined features, too perfect to be mistaken for a human, hide a wild, predatory power that will knock your socks off before you can take a breath. A demigod, descendant of Ares, god of war, he makes his ancestor proud with his handsome face, chestnut hair, and deep brown eyes.

"Sit!" he barks, and I almost jump out of my skin.

Lowering gingerly at the edge of the already uncomfortable chair, I sit ramrod straight, still staring at his chin. It's an excellent chin, don't get me wrong, but it's definitely not that fascinating that I keep staring at it. The slight smirk that fleets his face tells me as much. Jerking my eyes to the desk, I grip the sides of the chair so I keep my smartass mouth in check. This is not the time to blurt out the first thing that comes to my mind, a trait I often can't control well. Minutes tick by, the struggle with my panic turning into anger.

"I told you the truth of what happened." Pushing the words through my clenched teeth, I finally meet his gaze. My chin juts out defiantly at his calm perusal.

"The shifter got away. He was your target." Leaning his forearms on the desk, his eyes bore into mine. "I have told you many times. You follow orders, do you understand?"

"You would've done the same thing if you were there." Holding onto my courage with everything in me, I don't look away. "I can still hear the terror in that scream. I have no clue what that thing was, but I've never seen anything like it."

"Where are your weapons?" I was hoping with all the shit tonight he wouldn't notice. I should've known better.

"I did not carry weapons on me tonight." Not wanting to give him time to ask questions, I continue talking, changing the subject. "No weapon I own would've helped tonight. I think whatever that thing is, it's not going to just leave. I can feel that we have a big problem on our hands."

"Shadows, you said?" He searches my face, and I let him see the fear I've been pushing aside.

"Like a shadow." Punctuating that I'm not sure what the hell it is, I force myself to look through the memory closely. "There were two of them before they merged into one. And I could tell when it had its attention on me. Definitely sentient and deadly."

"A mist..." His chocolate-brown eyes narrow, while his deep voice trails off, sending a nervous flutter through my chest that short-circuits my brain.

"And the shifter said he didn't kill the witch, he found

her already dead before the call came in." I have no idea why I poked that bear, and I want to kick myself.

"You had time to chat with it?" One perfectly shaped eyebrow lifts in question.

"If you call him planting a boot in my face chatting, sure." Shrugging a shoulder, my fingers grip the sides of the chair so tight I can hear the wood groaning.

"What am I going to do with you, Drake?" Leaning back in his comfy chair, Andrius folds his fingers over his flat stomach.

"Let me go home to take a shower and get some sleep?" Tilting my head, my vision blurs imagining doing just that. "Some food will be nice, too," I add wistfully.

"I blame this on your mixed heritage." Scowling at me, his lips press in a thin line. "Your powers are clashing, distracting you. This was your last try to prove I didn't make a mistake by giving you a chance. Not even my curiosity on figuring you out can last forever."

"I'm not trying to get my ass out of trouble, Andrius." At his sharp look, I backpedal really fast. "Boss...Mr. Roberti, Sir." Ending it with a groan, I cover my face with my hands. "I'm blowing this up big time." My words are muffled through my fingers.

Roberti grunts, agreeing that I'm only digging a deeper hole for myself. At least he is not quiet. That's when I'm ready to pee my pants, when he says nothing. Removing my hands from my face, I fill my lungs and release the breath I'm holding, slowly locking my eyes on his again. The moment of truth has come, and there is no delaying the inevitable. It's my only chance right now if I want to stay in the Agency.

Honesty.

Secret Origins

"Okay, listen." The jackhammering of my heart against my ribs makes me sound breathless and on the verge of tears. "Three weeks ago, some new power started manifesting. Its bursts of energy come and go as they please, and I can't control it. It makes me zone out at times, not to a point where I have no idea what I'm doing or where I am. It's more like my mind wanders off at awkward moments. It doesn't happen often." I rush to assure him before he tells me to get lost. "But it does happen, and that's the reason I've screwed up a few times. On the bright side, it helps when I use it on anyone. It paralyzes them long enough that they can be incapacitated...if it lasts longer than a few seconds."

"Your mother is a pure-blooded vampire," Roberti says pointedly.

"I didn't notice," I reply dryly by default and bite the inside of my mouth the same second. *What the hell is wrong with you Franky!* I scream at myself internally.

"And your father, a pure-blooded Fae." Andrius narrows his eyes at me again, turning them into slits. "Or so all of you say."

"Excuse me? What's that supposed to mean?" Anger bubbles up inside me just like every time my parents are mentioned, especially after my father was killed.

"These new powers could be coming from his side." His words would've been comforting if not for the calculating look in his gaze while he stares at me like I'm a bug under a microscope. "You should've come to me the moment this happened."

"I thought I had it under wraps." The shrug I give him is not intentional, it's like a twitch my body is making out of my control. "Obviously, I was wrong."

"You are going to go home and stay home"—His eyes

bore into mine, the power punch to obey him almost doubling me over— "until I tell you to come back."

"I just need food, a shower, and a good night sleep. Not necessarily in that order either. I'll be as good as new in the morning." A weight lifts off my chest. He is not kicking me out.

I got excited too soon.

"You are suspended until further notice." My mouth opens to argue my case, but it's left hanging, "Get out!"

I realize I didn't say a word back to him when I'm standing outside the building in front of my bike. Scrubbing a hand over my face, my head hangs down on my shoulders. There is nothing I can do to change his mind right now, so I better head home. Yanking the full-face helmet off the handle, I shove it over my head, slapping the top of it with my palm a couple of times. I push the visor down after I straddle the Ducati, the purring of the beast between my legs not soothing me as it usually does.

"Fuck!" The bike wobbles slightly when I slam my palm on it a few times in anger.

With nothing else left to do and a dread taking residence in my chest, I rev the engine before skidding out of the parking lot like the hounds of Hell are on my tail.

Investigated: Chapter Three

The chatter is a distant hum assaulting my ears as I stare into nothing above the wall full of liquor bottles at the bar. It has been four days since I got suspended and I think I started going insane inside my one-bedroom apartment. The first two days, I only slept, ate, and then slept some more. Those are a blur, and I think I didn't even take a shower. The third day I got pissed off at myself, so I might've broken a few things when I chucked them at the wall. The hallway might also have a fist-size hole next to my bedroom door, but nobody needs to know about that.

To break the insanity before I destroy everything I own —although I don't own much—tonight I dress up and take myself to Raven's Feather, a pub owned by my friend. My only friend, actually, Daren. He is a mage that wants nothing to do with his kind, so he started his own business in the middle of town. Having to hide what I am doesn't make me a social butterfly, so I usually stay away from everyone. Physical touch is something I find repulsive most of the time. My skin is too sensitive, almost like a magnet sucking in whatever the person is feeling at the moment. Not that anyone will touch me, not if they know I am a hybrid. They'll come for my head.

But not Daren.

We crossed paths while I was angry at the world for being a freak, and he was just as angry for losing the woman he loved. She was a hybrid as well, and when the Mages found out, they had her killed, then branded Daren as a traitor. No one is allowed to hide a hybrid. Well, unless you are Andrius, in which case they all turn to look the other way.

The sigil marking Daren is displayed on top of his left hand like a black stamp. He wears it proudly, which is the main reason I actually spoke to him the first time I saw him. Our mutual dislike of the entitled pure bloods, as well as him not hitting on me, made us fast friends.

As unfortunate or as heart breaking as his fate is, and he loves to tell the story often, it kinda worked out well for him. Not being associated with any species, in particular, gained him quite a clientele and a badass reputation to boot. He does not tolerate any bullshit, and has no problem using his magic on anyone. Everyone is welcomed here as long as they follow the rules.

No killing inside the pub.

That's it. As soon as you leave the door, you're on your own. Luckily, Daren has pretty good wards around the place, so it's kinda safe-ish to get to your ride without a problem. Also having the higher-ups visiting has made it a less likely spot to get murdered. All in all, not bad for a town full of supernaturals running on instinct more than rational thought.

"You want another one, or are you going to milk that one all night?" Daren comes to the corner of the bar where

I'm hugging the beer between my palms like it's my precious.

"You buying?" Lifting an eyebrow in challenge, I chug half the beer down my throat.

"Sure." Smirking, he keeps rubbing the glass in his hands with a rag. "If you tell me why you're more prickly than usual."

"I'm not prickly." My mouth twists in a grimace after I snap at him. "Okay fine, I'm prickly, but when I have a reason to be."

"If you say so." His dark brown hair flops over his forehead, and he jerks his head to move it out of his green eyes. Amusement is dancing in his gaze when my eyes narrow at him. "A beer for your thoughts." He chuckles.

"It's a penny for your thoughts, jackass." Sipping the beer, my attention goes over his shoulder as I look at everyone behind me through the mirrored wall.

"Pennies don't work on you." Still chuckling, he grabs a large, frosted mug, filling it up from the tap.

"Touché, my friend." Pointing my beer bottle at him, my lips twitch, but I can't find enough strength to smile.

Daren slams the mug full of beer on the bar, snatching the now empty bottle from my hand. Leaning his hip across from me, his arms fold over his chest. I know the look on his face, and I'm really not in the mood to talk about my problems, but I can tell he is not going to leave me be until I tell him why I'm sitting here instead of chasing some asshole through the streets of Sienna.

"I got suspended."

Grab your copy...
vinci-books.com/investigated

About the Author

Maya Daniels, USA Today Bestselling and multi-award-winning supernatural suspense author, is a fun-loving woman with many talents.

She traveled the world, gaining life experiences that helped her career as an investigative journalist, as well as her storytelling. Maya writes compelling tales of magic, mythical creatures, loyalty, and life-changing friendships with snarky female characters—much like herself.

Her travels have taken her to Europe, Africa, Asia, Australia, and America. Born with her feet in motion, she currently resides in Ohio, spinning her next epic story that you will not want to put down.

Her biggest 'sins' are her love of chocolate and coffee—through an IV drip! One to never sit still, Maya practices Reiki healing, different types of martial arts, reads about the arcane, talks to furry creatures more than humans, picks up a sledgehammer for home improvement, and travels with her fated mate, seeking her own adventures.

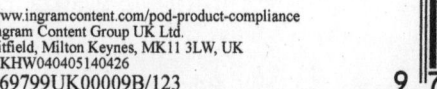